MW00907639

To order additional copies of
Not Alone, by Cheryl Porter,
call **1-800-765-6955**.

Visit us at
www.reviewandherald.com
for information on other Review and Herald® products.

CHERYL PORTER

NOT *Alone*

Battling
the Devil
in the
City
of Angels

R
REVIEW AND HERALD® PUBLISHING ASSOCIATION
Since 1861 www.reviewandherald.com

Copyright © 2009 by Cheryl D. Porter

Published by Review and Herald® Publishing Association, Hagerstown, MD
21741-1119

All rights reserved. No portion of this book may be reproduced, stored in a retrieval
system, or transmitted in any form or by any means (electronic, mechanical, photo-
copy, recording, scanning, or other), except for brief quotations in critical reviews or
articles, without the prior written permission of the publisher.

Review and Herald® titles may be purchased in bulk for educational, business, fund-
raising, or sales promotional use. For information, e-mail SpecialMarkets@reviewand
herald.com

The Review and Herald® Publishing Association publishes biblically based materials
for spiritual, physical, and mental growth and Christian discipleship.

All texts are from the *Holy Bible, New International Version.* Copyright © 1973, 1978,
1984, International Bible Society. Used by permission of Zondervan Bible Publishers.

The author assumes full responsibility for the accuracy of all facts and quotations as
cited in this book.

This book was
Edited by Richard Coffen
Copyedited by James Cavil
Cover designed by Ron J. Pride
Cover photo by: Stockbyte
Interior designed by Heather Rogers
Typeset: Bembo 12/14

PRINTED IN U.S.A.

13 12 11 10 09   5 4 3 2 1

Library of Congress Cataloging-in-Publication Data

Porter, Cheryl, 1958-   .
  Not alone: battling the devil in the city of angels / Cheryl Porter.
    p. cm.
  Summary: In 1970s Los Angeles a lonely teenager named Kellie struggles with
the temptations of alcohol, drugs, and the occult, until an older Christian friend in-
troduces her to God.
  [1. Loneliness—Fiction. 2. Occultism—Fiction. 3. Seventh-day Adventists—
Fiction. 4. Christian life—Fiction. 5. Los Angeles (Calif.)—History—20th cen-
tury—Fiction.] I. Title.
  PZ7.P8245No 2009
  [Fic]—dc22

                                                    2009009414

ISBN 978-0-8280-2471-6

To my children,

Lisa and Devin

For their **unconditional love**

and **support,**

and for

cheering me on when

I needed it most.

Contents

Chapter 1

Dark Roots

"Remember, Kellie, have dinner ready by 6:00," Mom called over her shoulder. "You know how cranky Dad gets when it's late. I'll be home to eat with you."

Mom was leaving for her job at the community college. Eleven-year-old Kellie pushed long strands of light-brown hair from her hazel eyes and watched Mom drive away in her station wagon. Dad was already at work, up at the nuclear rocket-testing site. Her 16-year-old brother, Tommy, was still in bed.

Kellie swallowed the last bite of cereal and went to her room to read. Somewhere in the house the air-conditioner kicked on, promising another long, hot summer day.

Hours later she ditched the book on ghost sightings and haunted houses to wander through their large ranch-style Los Angeles home. Tommy had slept late and then left with friends. Feeling abandoned, Kellie wondered how she could fill the empty hours.

In the kitchen she poured ice water and re-membered with longing the yam tarts their maid, Maria, used to make for her. That was before her parents' purchase of a new custom-built, white-and-gold camper van. That meant the maid had to go. Now Kellie made dinner during the week *and* cleaned the swimming pool, pulled weeds, made beds, and straightened her room. Tommy worked too, doing dishes, cleaning house, and mowing the lawn. On weekends they both helped Dad with big-ger projects. She often wondered what just being a kid—with a mom at home and fewer chores—would feel like.

She flipped on the television, but nothing good was on. Besides, the den felt creepy with its collec-tion of foreign statues, especially the one with too many hands.

Moving on, she ambled to the living room to look at books and photo albums. She enjoyed both, but disliked that room more than the den. Above the couch hung a large painting of what Tommy called a pinup girl, her smile prideful, eyes mean. There were other paintings from her parents' travels that bothered her too, including jungle scenes with people doing embarrassing things, but none were as yucky as the pinup girl.

Ignoring the painting, she took a photo album back to her room. Maybe studying her ancestors would pass the time. As she turned the pages, her guinea pigs, Fred and Harriet, played in their cage, running in circles, squeaking.

"Harriet, calm down," Kellie laughed. The brown rodent stopped short, nose twitching, whiskers quivering. Then she sneezed from the dust they'd made and started eating.

Bored, Kellie closed the album and looked critically around the room. It was decorated with toy horses, her mom's porcelain geisha doll, a fat Buddha, a farm mural she'd helped her dad paint on two walls, and orange-flowered curtains chosen and put up while Kellie was away having her tonsils out. The room wasn't ugly. It just didn't look much like a girl's room. Not that it mattered. The prettiest girl's room ever wouldn't take away the bored frustration, the sense that her constant aloneness meant she was completely unimportant.

Grabbing the house key, she decided to escape on her bike for a while.

Next door, Mrs. Mills looked beautiful as she busily watered her petunias. Younger than Kellie's mom and very stylish, Mrs. Mills' fancy hairstyle and clothes were her trademark.

"Morning, Kellie," she called out.

Kellie waved before taking off down the street, first pretending the bike was a speeding car, then a galloping horse on the trail. It was fun . . . but not enough.

What she needed was a friend, but the girls from school didn't seem to like her much anymore. It could be her shyness, but Kellie thought it was more likely her hair and clothes that were all wrong. When she was little, her older sister, Ellen, had fixed her hair. But then Ellen had moved away, and Kellie was just no good at doing her own.

Biting her lip, she focused now on whom she could play with. Her mind turned to Beth . . . she'd been nice to Kellie all through sixth grade. Turning the bike sharply, she pedaled hard toward Beth's house.

Once there, she rode in circles, stalling. *What if she already has a friend over?* she worried. Part of her wanted to run home. But then she remembered the emptiness, and courageously rang the doorbell.

Beth's mom answered, smiling and wiping floury hands on a blue apron.

"She's in her room," she said, pointing down the hall. "Go on back. I'll bring you girls a snack."

Kellie stepped inside. The house smelled of baking cookies. Shuffling down the hall, she stopped at Beth's door and knocked. Hearing nothing, she called, "Beth, it's Kellie. May I come in?"

She heard movement before the door flew open.

"Hi!" Beth exclaimed, amber eyes blinking. Her dark-brown hair was combed back in a ponytail, every hair in place, and tied with a white ribbon. "I didn't know you were coming! Here, sit down. I'm doing my favorite puzzle. See, it has horses and a red barn."

She made space on the floor while Kellie looked around in awe. The room had rose-patterned wallpaper, ruffled white curtains, and a white four-poster bed covered with a pink bedspread, dolls, and stuffed animals. It was beautiful.

"Your mom's bringing food," Kellie offered.

"Great, I'm starved." Beth was already searching for another piece. "So what are you doing today?"

"I was bike riding and it got hot. I thought maybe we could go swimming at my house."

"That sounds fun, but I'll have to ask my mom."

The early afternoon passed quickly as they played and munched warm cookies. When they'd finished assembling the puzzle, Beth left to ask her mother about swimming.

Moments later she returned, looking disappointed.

"I can't," she explained. "I guess the other moms told mine that your parents are never home and your house has weird stuff in it that I shouldn't see, whatever that means. Sorry, Kellie . . . I really wanted to go."

Kellie blushed, fighting back tears. No one had asked her to leave, but she was too humiliated to stay. She raced home, tears blinding her all the way. *Beth's right*, she thought. *No one's waiting to watch me swim or bring lemonade, or anything. It's not fair!*

She spent the late afternoon floating in the pool, forming a plan before obediently making dinner and serving it on TV trays. Afterward, Tommy cleaned up and Dad watched another show while he drank an entire bottle of wine before switching to vodka. Mom graded papers in her office.

Putting the plan into action, Kellie boldly approached her mother's cluttered desk.

"Mom, can we hire a maid for the rest of the summer so I can have friends over? I hate being alone every day."

"You can have friends here anytime," she said, not looking up. "You don't need a maid for that."

Kellie shook her head.

"You don't understand! I invited Beth today. Her mom said no because there are no adults here." Her voice was trembling. "All the moms feel that way."

Her mom looked up and frowned. Her pale-blue eyes behind the glasses were weary, and her short, graying perm made her look older.

"I'm sorry," she said. Her voice sounded tired. "We can't afford a maid anymore. Besides, you kids are old enough to get by on your own. Pretty soon those moms will come around. You'll see. In the meantime, play at their houses."

Without another word, Kellie walked away. Nothing at home was going to change. Back in her room she clicked on the radio. In a month she'd be starting junior high. Maybe then she'd meet someone like her, someone who needed a friend too.

Chapter 2

Summer's End

Standing before the closet, Kellie eagerly gave the new dresses, jeans, and tops a careful inspection. The last month had dragged by with little to break up the boredom. Now summer was over, and tomorrow was the start of seventh grade. She just had to wear the perfect outfit.

Looking everything over, she chose the short olive-green dress. The color matched her eyes, and the cut flattered her slim figure. She was pulling it out for one last try-on when Dad came stomping down the hall, making her stomach lurch.

"Where's your mother?" he bellowed, his large body filling the doorframe. "She needs to hear this too."

"I don't know," Kellie answered, too scared to ask why. She could tell he'd been drinking.

He stayed put, face red, hands jammed on hips. After a torturous silence, he stuck his head into the hallway and hollered for Mom, never leaving his spot.

Moments later she joined them.

"What's all the noise about?" she asked, looking from one to the other.

He raked his curly salt-and-pepper hair and pointed a shaking finger at the closet.

"Do you have any idea what you two have been spending on clothes?" he demanded. "I was going over the checkbook and couldn't believe it! You've spent a fortune! Why does she need so much? We're not made of money, you know." He angrily crossed his arms over a rounded tummy and frowned, fuming.

Kellie stared at the green dress and felt sick. It *had* been kind of expensive. Mom had bought matching sandals to go with it too. Making a quick mental inventory, she remembered all their other purchases: gym clothes, sneakers, a winter coat, stockings, a purse for her house key and lunch money, notebooks, pencils . . . it suddenly seemed endless. Dad was right. They probably had spent way too much money.

She shot her mom a glance and waited. For a long moment no one said anything. In the silence Kellie noticed odd sounds: a car starting somewhere outside, the loud ticking of her little heart-shaped clock, the noisy slurps Fred made drinking from his water bottle.

This was her parents' pattern . . . Mom would make a decision, Dad would drink too much alcohol, and they'd fight. Then Mom would grudgingly offer a submissive apology to calm his anger. Kellie was imagining what this next apology would sound like when Mom surprised everyone. She straightened her shoulders and returned Dad's steady gaze. She looked anything *but* apologetic.

"Kellie's grown up a lot since last year," she said, her voice respectful yet firm. "She's become a young lady and needed new clothes for seventh grade. I know they were expensive, but there's nothing she or I can do about the cost of clothes. Anyway, she assures me she won't need any more for quite a while. Right, Kellie?"

She couldn't believe her ears. Mom had stood up for her! She could tell Dad was surprised too. He just stood there, chin jutting, eyes blinking, looking stumped.

"Well?" Mom prompted. "Tell him what you told me."

Kellie forced herself to look him in the eye.

"I *love* my new clothes, Dad. I won't ask for any more. Honest." She watched his face relax a little. "Besides, I think I'm done growing . . . even my feet have stopped getting bigger."

He rolled his eyes and walked away, grumbling and shaking his head all the way down the hall. The argument was over.

Kellie sighed with relief and brushed lint specks off the green dress. It was still her favorite, but now it made her feel guilty, as if it represented all that was wrong with her life. She heard someone else sigh and realized Mom was still there, waiting. She looked up and their eyes met. Suddenly Kellie's filled with tears. Dad's words, even the roll of his dark eyes, had hurt.

"Come here," Mom said, offering a hug. "Don't pay him any mind when he's like that. He doesn't re-ally expect you to start school wearing old clothes. By tomorrow he'll have forgotten all about it. You should too. OK?"

Kellie nodded, but the tears kept coming. Then her mom surprised her again by staying long enough to help plan the next day, including how to wear her hair and what time to wake up so she wouldn't be late for school.

Later that evening she sat alone in the kitchen consoling herself with ice cream, taking mental stock of her family . . . comparing her parents with others she knew.

Besides the fact that her mom worked while most moms stayed home, her parents were *much older* than most other parents. This wasn't their fault, of course, but it was sometimes embarrassing for Kellie.

Their family didn't go to church, either. Most of the families she knew, including her aunt Betty, uncle Winn, and all their relatives back East, did. Her parents lived by their own rules; in the summertime they didn't even bother with pajamas—much to Kellie's distaste. Likewise, they didn't make many rules for her and Tommy, either. Not that she wanted more rules . . . she just didn't understand why her parents thought they weren't needed.

Even holidays were different at their house. When other girls bought new Easter dresses, Kellie's mom said they were silly. And every Christmas she had to go to someone else's house to touch and smell a real Christmas tree or hear carols, because her parents cared only about buying presents and eating a big dinner.

Taking a bite of rocky road ice cream, she shook her head. Feeling different might be OK if their family had a good reason, but Kellie couldn't find one.

"Hey, Squirt, why the long face?" It was Tommy.

He was already taller than their dad, lean-muscled and tanned from being on the swim team. Hovering over her, he eyed the half-finished dessert.

She snatched it from his reach.

"Oh, come on, just a bite," he teased.

"Get your own."

He ran a lazy hand through thick black hair and threw her an amused wink, his dark eyes glinting with mischief. Then he fetched his own ice cream and joined her.

"I hear Mom and Dad got into it today."

"Yeah. He was mad about my new clothes."

"Don't let it get to you, kid. Just think, you'll be starting junior high tomorrow . . . that's pretty exciting. You'll be meeting new people and going to different classes. Don't let him spoil it."

"Thanks," she said, wondering why he was being so nice.

Switching off the light, Kellie lay in bed and imagined what school would be like. Would she get lost trying to find her classes? What if she forgot her locker combination? Even though they didn't spend much time together anymore, the plan was to walk to school with her oldest friend, Heather. But they might not have the same classes, and the prospect of hundreds of new classmates was terrifying.

Diving under the blanket, she squeezed her eyes shut and waited for morning.

Chapter 3

The Invitation

Kellie spent that first morning racing from class to class, never sure where to go next. Before school, she'd carefully fixed her hair with a barrette. By lunchtime the heat and frantic rushing had loosened it, allowing hair to fall in her eyes and every other direction. She'd forgotten a comb, so repairs weren't possible.

Defeated, she yanked the barrette out and tossed it into her purse. Other girls walking by still looked well-groomed and fresh. She wondered how they managed it. There must have been an instruction book that she'd missed on the way to seventh grade.

She followed the crowd toward the cafeteria and felt comforted by the aroma of macaroni and cheese. She was eager to buy some until she saw the long line. Then she wished she'd brown-bagged it.

"Heather!" she called out, waving to her friend near the front of the line. The girl never turned around. She was busy twirling her long blond hair around her finger, talking to someone Kellie didn't know.

When Kellie finally had her meal, all the lunch tables were full. She settled beneath a tree outside and wondered if anyone would notice her solitude. Tommy was wrong. This wasn't fun at all!

Weeks later she busied herself staring away from the teacher, Miss Todd, waiting for science to end. It was her final class period, and she wanted to go home.

"Can anyone explain the evolution theory?" Miss Todd repeated, pacing and tapping chalk against her plump hand.

Kellie knew the theory well. As an anthropology professor, her mom had often explained how evolutionists believed the earth had evolved over millions of years to eventually support life. Her dad, a nuclear engineer, believed in evolution too. But Kellie had trouble believing in things that supposedly happened eons before human beings came into existence. How could anyone know for sure? So she ignored the question until the bell finally rang. She was heading for the door when a hand stopped her. It was Jennifer, a girl she barely knew.

"Hey," she said. "Have a sec?" Her unruly red curls framed friendly green eyes.

"Sure."

"My church youth group meets tomorrow night. If you like, my mom and I could pick you up. Want to come?"

Kellie hesitated. Nobody had ever invited her to church, not even Heather.

"I'll have to ask my mom. Can I tell you tomorrow?"

"OK. See you then."

Kellie left the campus quickly to walk home alone. She'd gone about a block when she noticed Jake and Scott walking on the opposite side of the street. Both boys were in her grade, and they were very popular. When Jake smiled at her, she panicked and sped up, never seeing the hole in the sidewalk. A second later she was flat on her stomach, books scattered.

Hating herself for her failure to look and her ultimate stumble, she peeked in their direction, hoping they hadn't seen. They had. Without a word she picked herself up and continued on, deliberately slowing down enough to let them get way ahead.

By the time she reached the corner house, her blush of embarrassment had faded. In the yard she was glad to see a friendly, familiar face.

"Hi," Mr. Hunnicut called out. He was pruning roses.

She offered the retired actor a shy wave. Even among the flowers, he resembled the crusty cowboy characters he'd played in the movies, right down to his graying hair and beard.

"How are you?" he asked. "School done for today?"

She nodded yes, but didn't stop to talk. She'd known him since kindergarten and liked him, but even he made her tongue-tied.

At the house she unlocked the door and dumped her books, then made a quick snack and settled cross-legged in front of the television. Pretty soon she was laughing at the antics on *Gilligan's Island,* happier than she'd been all day. But when it ended and she'd finished her snack, she had to turn her attention to homework and chores.

She spread her books and assignments out on the bed and got busy. By the time both math and science were finished, Kellie had just a few minutes left to relax and think about Jennifer's invitation before she needed to make dinner.

It would be neat to have a new friend. Heather and the other girls she'd known in elementary school had obviously moved on to other friendships this year. It used to be fun going to slumber parties at Heather's house, staying up late while they took turns telling ghost stories and talking about boys. But now she couldn't remember the last time Heather had called. They didn't even walk to school together anymore. Heather had found a new friend to walk with.

Kellie closed her eyes and tried to imagine Jennifer's church. She'd never been inside one. She pictured a plain room filled with kids, all looking at her. *What does a church youth group do, anyway?* she wondered. *Will it cost money? What if they don't like me?*

The whole idea of religion was a mystery. Ever since she could remember, her parents had claimed not to believe in God. They said only science could explain the world, the planets, and the vast emptiness beyond the stars. Life to them was temporary, like the life of an animal or a bug. It had a beginning, work in between, and an end, but nothing after that. Kellie, more creative than scientific, wasn't so sure.

Sometimes she'd sit in the backyard after dark and look at the stars, wondering how they'd got there and what was behind them, and behind *that*. Earth and its solar system couldn't have come from nothing. Didn't there have to be something, or *someone*, creating everything, the same way she loved to create drawings on blank paper? But who? He'd have to be awfully big and powerful to make what she couldn't even see.

In her whole life there'd been just one time she'd thought that *maybe* there was a God who watched over and cared for people. It happened during a family visit to Bodie State Historic Park, a real gold-mining ghost town in California. She'd foolishly gone exploring alone and wound up in a far-off cabin where the backroom floor had caved in. She'd crept back outside, expecting the floor beneath her to collapse any moment. It never did.

The memory made her wonder if God had kept her safe that day and if that meant He really did exist. Feeling curious, she remembered Grandma's old Bible still tucked in the living room bookshelf. She ran to get it, opening its latch to reveal dusty pages. The pictures were pretty, but the print was too tiny and the words too old-fashioned to understand. Disappointed, she put it back. If she did go with Jennifer, maybe someone there could explain about God.

That night Mom praised her cooking.

"Delicious," she said. "Homework all done?"

Kellie nodded and mentioned Jennifer's invitation.

"Do you want to go?"

"Maybe."

"Well, you know how I feel about churches. But it's up to you."

Kellie watched Mom head to her office. Dad and Tommy had already gone in opposite directions. She still felt like talking about it, but there was no one to talk to. Tommy didn't understand her shyness anyway.

So it was up to her. She yearned to accept, to show Jennifer she wanted to be friends . . . but she doubted if she had the courage to go through with it.

Chapter 4

Mexico Christmas

By the next day Kellie's shyness had won. She just couldn't bring herself to say yes. Jennifer took it well, but Kellie felt sad she'd missed out on a new friend. For the rest of that school year she tried making the best of things. But when summer came, she joyfully abandoned shoes and notebooks and forgot school until hot Santa Ana winds and new school supplies announced eighth grade had arrived.

That first week she hoped school might be different than before, but the circles of friends remained tight and the assignments tougher than ever. There was one bright spot, her three-dimensional art class, where her talents really shined. But the rest of the first semester made her long for Christmas vacation.

Kellie awoke from a nap feeling groggy. Her face was sore from the scratchy camper upholstery, her skin sweaty and her stomach queasy. The family had decided they'd drive to Mexico City for Christmas to visit friends. Unfortunately, a heat wave had struck, and Kellie had come down with the flu. Tommy had escaped the long trek by landing his first job, and had stayed home.

Rubbing her eyes, Kellie noticed her mom watching her from up front.

"How're you feeling?" Mom asked.

"Lousy."

She nodded sympathetically.

"We'll reach Mexico City by sunset. If you don't feel better by morning, I'll find a doctor."

Kellie shook her head. She didn't want some strange doctor examining her.

"I'll be better," she promised. "I just need to stop moving."

Minutes later Dad pulled over so Mom could drive and Kellie could stretch her legs and move to the front seat. After that, her stomach settled down enough to let her relax and read.

As afternoon wore on, the sky grew dark with clouds. Kellie opened her window to feel the cool wind and smell the approaching rain. She enjoyed the change in weather until the storm suddenly broke with a loud clap of thunder overhead.

She rolled the window back up and watched as huge tumbleweeds blew across the road in swirls of blinding dust. Then the clouds burst, dumping sheets of heavy rain, blurring the windshield and soaking the road. Booming thunder and searing lightning gave her goose bumps.

Not Alone

Despite the growing danger, she felt no fear until driving conditions turned treacherous: the rapid buildup of rain and mud on the asphalt caused their tires to lose traction, sending the camper skidding sideways toward oncoming traffic.

Kellie screamed.

"Quiet!" Mom ordered.

Kellie slapped her mouth shut and stared as her mother struggled to control the van. She wanted to yell for help, but there was no one to call upon. Tears of terror filled her eyes.

They were about to hit a pickup truck when their tires unexpectedly held and turned . . . only to skid again in the opposite direction toward an old barn. They slid closer and closer, almost touching the fence before skidding off in yet another direction, this time in the direction of a crowded bus. Kellie couldn't watch anymore . . . and hid behind trembling hands, waiting for the crash. But instead of twisting metal, she heard Mom's relieved sigh and felt the van roll gently to a stop. Kellie peeked to make sure . . . yes, they were safe!

"Everyone OK?" Mom asked.

Dad said he was fine.

Outside, the storm began to wind down. Mom waited a moment, gave her permed hair a pat, and shifted into drive. "Danger's over," she announced. "Time to get moving."

Kellie couldn't be that calm. Her stomach clenched with a fresh wave of nausea.

That night she gratefully crawled into bed while her parents ate supper and talked. They had parked on a quiet street in the humble neighborhood of their friends,

Mr. and Mrs. Cortez, in the heart of Mexico City.

The next morning Kellie awoke alone. The warm air and lively street noises told her it was late. She dressed quickly and stepped out into bright sunshine, feeling miraculously well and happy to be alive. Unsure where to go, she approached a nearby iron gate. Her dad had pointed it out the night before, and she hoped it would lead to the Cortez home.

Its rusty hinges complained at her gentle push but opened to reveal a long narrow walkway. Pausing, she heard faint, familiar voices drifting from the far end. She passed several tiny apartments before reaching another gate that led to the courtyard of a small adobe house protected by high cement walls topped with broken glass. Nearby, an old woman washed clothes on a scrub board in a metal tub. She stopped to smile and pointed inside. Through open windows Kellie could see her parents with the Cortez family. She fought her usual shyness and went inside.

The clay walls kept the house deliciously cool. The rooms were clean and colorfully decorated. It was pleasant, but to her American eyes everything looked primitive. The floors consisted of stone and cement, the furniture was handmade, and the kitchen looked bare, with only a few doorless cupboards and a large plank table. There was no stove, only an open hearth outside for cooking.

Despite all that, the table overflowed with appetizing home-cooked food.

"That looks really good," she said. "I'm starved!"

"You're feeling better?" her mom asked.

"I am. No doctor for me."

After brunch they went sightseeing before returning for a Christmas Eve feast. At midnight 15-year-
old Victor Cortez invited Kellie's family to Mass.

"Dad and I will stay here," Mom said, squeezing
Kellie's hand. "But you go. It might be interesting."

This time she accepted, determined not to miss
out again.

The night air felt warm as they walked two
blocks. The open windows of the old church glowed
with candlelight spilling onto the sidewalk as bells
rang in the steeple. Worshippers filled the sanctuary
and its entrance to overflowing.

Undaunted, Kellie politely pushed farther inside
until someone passed her a candle and she could see
the white-robed priest speaking behind a large Bible.
She couldn't understand his words, but felt them as
waves of emotion spread through the crowd, filling
her with an unexplainable happiness.

When the Mass ended, an old man played the an-
tiquated organ while people slowly filed out. Kellie
stayed put, clutching her candle and taking it all in.
The worshippers' faces glowed with joy. She didn't
want to leave. Not yet.

When the church was nearly empty, she reluctantly let Victor walk her back while she contem-
plated all she'd just seen, heard, and felt. It seemed to
her that the Bible lay at the heart of faith. But was
what the Bible said real or just made-up fables? She
remembered their near-crash the day before. Had that
been like her adventure in Bodie? Had God saved her
from tragedy . . . again? Someday she hoped to find
the facts, if there were any, behind faith.

Chapter 5

The Challenge

Back from Christmas vacation, Kellie readjusted to life in Los Angeles. She did her best to handle classes and homework, but life at home only got harder as Dad's drinking grew worse, Mom's work took up more time, and Tommy split his time between work and friends. Kellie still wanted to explore the question of faith, but the opportunity never came up. She found it hard enough to face each moment as it came.

Despite the prospect of spending more time at home, she was glad when summer came. This year she'd decided to make use of her solitude. Lazing by the pool would include studying teen magazines to learn tips on clothes, grooming, even how to make conversation. Time in her room would involve practicing hair styles and planning her fall wardrobe.

By the time summer break ended, she felt much better about starting ninth grade, and it didn't take long for her summer investment to pay off. Her new look and attitude soon brought new friends, including a best friend, Mary. Kellie's final year of junior high flew by in a haze of school projects, glee club concerts, and a class trip to Disneyland.

After graduation Mary talked Kellie into taking Scottish Highland dancing lessons. The plan was for both of them to make the high school marching band's team of Highland dancers. On the first night of class Kellie stood beside Mary in a room full of girls, straining to point her toes out, tuck her bottom under, push her shoulders back, keep her head high, and hold her hands and arms just *so*.

"This is impossible!" she giggled. "I can't do it all at once!"

"I know!" Mary moaned, struggling to hold the same pose. She was tall and slim and looked like a ballerina, but she lacked the grace of a dancer.

"Remember, girls, your school tryouts are in August." The teacher, Mrs. Pruitt, turned stern gray eyes toward Kellie. "Only *four* of you will be chosen for the team."

Kellie gulped and raised her arms higher. She knew her chances were slim . . . but the uniforms were *so* pretty, and the band got to travel and perform all over Los Angeles. Last year they'd even marched in the Rose Parade.

For the next few weeks she tried harder to point her toes and leap gracefully, but practicing on her own wasn't enough. One day Mary invited Kellie to spend the night so they could practice together. Her room was large, with lots of mirrors to show if their kicks and poses were right.

Mary danced first while Kellie watched from the floor. Leaning back, Kellie's hand accidentally touched a thick book. She reached over to move it out of the way and was surprised to see . . . a Bible.

"I didn't know you were Christian," Kellie observed, picking it up.

Mary held her pose long enough to shrug before leaping over an imaginary sword.

"Have been all my life," she said with a smile. "So is my family. It's just who we are . . . no big deal."

"It's a big deal to me," Kellie whispered with envy. She gently turned the pages, noticing that the words looked different from those in her grandmother's Bible.

"Hey, you're supposed to be watching me," Mary prodded. "Am I holding my arms right? What about my kicks? I don't think I'm doing them fast enough. What do you think?"

Kellie reluctantly abandoned the Holy Book to focus on Mary. When it was Kellie's turn to dance, Mary was so full of suggestions that Kellie finally gave up, plopping down in a frustrated heap.

"Need a break?" Mary asked.

Kellie nodded. It was obvious by her aching calf muscles and frequent mistakes that she lacked the talent needed for Highland dancing.

The girls went to make a snack. Mary's mom and older brother were in other parts of the house, working on projects, and her dad wouldn't get home until later. They had the kitchen to themselves.

Kellie sat on a barstool and watched Mary prepare fresh fruit and tall glasses of ice-cold milk. As Kellie thought back to the Bible, her mind overflowed with questions. "Mary," she finally ventured, "can I ask you something?"

"Sure." Her warm tone gave Kellie courage.

"I was wondering . . . how do you *know* the Bible is true? I mean, isn't it like really *old?* Do you even know who wrote it?"

As soon as the words were out, she wondered if she'd said the wrong thing. But she just had to know!

Mary brought over the food and sat down. Popping a peach slice in her mouth, she thoughtfully chewed while Kellie sampled the grapes and waited.

"I guess it's mostly faith," she said finally. "I just know in my heart that it's all true. But there have been studies and stuff to show that it's accurate. Did you know there are people who do nothing but study copies of the Bible that are thousands of years old? Anyway, my pastor says that a bunch of different authors wrote it at different times. But even if there wasn't proof, I'd still believe the Bible is real."

Kellie sipped her milk, considering Mary's words.

"But what does the Bible *do* for you? And it's so big! Have you ever read the whole thing?"

Mary laughed good-naturedly at Kellie's laundry list of questions, flashing a mouthful of braces.

"I've read a lot of it, but not the whole thing," she admitted. "Finishing it is one of my goals. And I guess I read it because it helps me figure things out, like when I'm sad or when stuff doesn't go my way. You should try it. It helps."

Kellie nodded, but knew she wouldn't. She didn't share her parents' evolutionist view of the world, but still needed something more to build her faith on than what Mary was offering. It was time to shift gears.

"Do you think we'll make the dance team?" she asked.

Mary swallowed the last drop of milk and shook her head.

"Probably not. Today was fun, but I don't think it helped much. We're both terrible."

Kellie carried her dishes to the sink and did a few dance steps along the way, almost tripping.

"You're right; we are!" she giggled.

That night they talked more about the upcoming tryouts. Before going to sleep, they agreed it was better to quit now and avoid the embarrassment of a competition.

With no more lessons to worry about, Kellie spent the rest of her summer happily goofing off with Mary and other friends until autumn came knocking again. But this time it was OK, because she had high school to look forward to. Despite not being a Highland dancer, she believed that this school year would be something special.

Chapter 6

Drill
Team

Tenth grade began with bus rides to and from
school, harder classes, and a lot more classmates
than junior high. The campus was bigger too, and everyone looked more grown-up. It was all very strange
and exciting, and so far, 15-year-old Kellie liked everything about it. Everything, that is, except gym
class.

For an hour every day, her classmates ran a mile
around the track and then practiced field exercises, including track hurdles and high bar vaulting. Kellie
hated all of it and showed no promise for improve-
ment. It was embarrassing. After several weeks the
class rotated to basketball, which was no better. In the
spring the worst was yet to come: softball.

Then Mary saved her.

"Hey," she said, catching up after a grueling game
of hoops. "Next semester, why don't we take drill
team for gym? All they do is practice routines . . . *no*

36

running or playing ball. And at the end they have try-outs for next year's team."

"Did you forget how bad we were at Highland dancing?"

"No . . . but maybe we'll be better at marching. If we make the team, we get to perform with the band at football games and parades, just like the dancers! If we don't, we've still gotten out of regular PE for the rest of the year."

So they gave drill team a try.

All that spring they practiced their marching skills and hung on their new gym teacher's every word. Miss Wang was young, energetic, and enthusiastic. To their great surprise, drill team turned out to be lots of fun and much easier than dance class! At home Kellie and Mary spent hours together trying new routines and memorizing drill patterns. In time they invited another friend, Cecelia, to join them as they practiced the competition routine to "Rock Around the Clock," the song everyone would use to compete.

Finally the big day came. When she spotted Mary in the tryout room, Kellie pulled her friend aside.

"I'm so nervous!" she whispered. "Do you think we have a chance?"

Mary flashed a Mona Lisa smile.

"I hope so . . . we worked as hard as we could. I *really* want this. Don't you?"

"Uh-huh," she breathed, rolling her eyes dramatically. "It's been *so* fun. I don't want it to end!"

Painfully aware that not everyone could make the team, they watched dozens of girls perform well for the squad leaders. When Kellie's turn came and the music started, she turned on her brightest smile and flew into the routine she'd memorized by heart. Every step was perfect, every position landed at exactly the right time in the song . . . until she accidentally dropped a pom-pom and fell out of step. For a split second she wanted to give up, end the routine in retreat. But then something happened: a source of strength she didn't know she possessed kicked in, putting sparkle back in her eyes and bounce in her step.

"Sorry!" she laughed graciously, scooping up the lost pom-pom and aiming a renewed smile at the young judges and Miss Wang. She caught up with the music and finished the routine perfectly.

Afterward she ran to Mary and hid her face.

"Oh, did you see *that*? Was I awful?"

"No," Mary whispered. "You finished, and that's what counts. Anyway, wish me luck! I'm up next."

Kellie cheered as Mary sailed through a flawless routine.

When it was all over, Kellie felt a deep sense of accomplishment. This time she'd faced her worst fears and given her best effort! But would it be enough?

For a week Kellie and Mary anguished over their performances. Then it was Friday, the day that all the girls who'd made drill team would be notified by noon of that fact through a flower ritual. As lunchtime approached, both girls sat anxiously through a lecture on poetry, very aware that many of the students in their fourth-period English class were either members of that year's drill team or were on the football team. They all knew about the ritual.

On one side of the room, Mary sat with her eyes fixed on the wall clock. Only 10 minutes remained in the period.

Over on her side, Kellie couldn't watch the clock anymore; she felt too much pressure. As she dropped her head onto folded arms, a slide show of old rejections filled her mind, causing even more doubt.

Then she heard a door creaking open, sneakered footsteps coming closer. A surge of hope coursed through her veins and quickened her pulse, and she lifted her head for one more attempt at acceptance.

A girl with a short Afro and skin the color of dark honey paused at Kellie's desk.

"Welcome to my squad, Kellie," the girl said with a beaming smile. She handed her a pale-pink rose. "Congratulations!"

Stunned, Kellie looked over to see Mary receiving a red rose from another smiling squad leader. A surge of happiness filled her whole being, spilling out in a rush of laughter as the entire class cheered and clapped for them both. In that unexpected moment of being respected by her peers, Kellie felt all those past hurts and unwanted memories fade blissfully away.

Kellie peered into her locker, finding things to throw away. It was finals week. Tenth grade was almost over.

While she tried to decide which drawings from art class to keep, someone tapped her arm. It was Cecelia.

Not Alone

"Hi," Kellie answered. She tossed a handful of sketches into a nearby trash can. "Guess I don't need them anymore. Think you'll miss this place over summer?"

"Maybe," Cecelia laughed, her round cheeks covered with freckles. "I'll miss my friends, for sure, and I can't wait to be on the drill team next year. Listen, I wanted to invite you to something. You know I belong to Job's Daughters, right? Well, we're having an important ceremony tomorrow night, and I'm allowed to bring a guest. Want to come?"

Kellie paused to consider her response. She still hated going places where she wouldn't know many people. But she didn't want to hurt her friend's feelings.

"OK," Kellie said with a nod. "Call me later with the details."

To her surprise, Kellie enjoyed the evening and wanted to learn more about the Freemasons religious order. The next day she caught up with Cecelia. "Hey, thanks for inviting me last night," she said. "It was fun. In fact, I was wondering if I could join Job's Daughters."

Cecelia looked surprised.

"No, Kellie . . . you can join only if someone in your family is a Mason. Sorry; I thought you knew."

"But I thought you said it was a *Christian* group."

"Well, sort of. But it's more like a club than a church. Anyway, I gotta go. See ya later . . . and have a great summer."

The unexpected rejection stung. *Someday*, Kellie thought to herself, *someday I'll find a way to God*.

Chapter 7

Big
Move

That summer brought family barbeques, home-made ice cream, and a long-overdue visit with Ellen, who was now married and living in another state. Tommy was shifting his attentions away from family as he started college and looked for a place of his own. Kellie, too, spent less time at home alone. The winds of change were stirring.

One afternoon Kellie took out her latest hobby, needlepoint. She was sorting her yarn when the door-bell rang. She looked through the small peephole and, deciding it would be OK, opened the door a crack, leaving the safety chain in place.

It was a balding, middle-aged man wearing a slightly wrinkled suit. He ran a handkerchief across his sweaty brow and offered a smile. "Excuse me, miss, could I speak with your mother?"

"She's . . . unavailable."

The man looked disappointed. "Ah, well, let me

leave this with you then." He offered a business card. "My name's Jack Anderson. I'm a real estate agent, looking for homes in the area to sell. Have your folks call me if they're interested."

She closed and locked the door and dropped it carelessly on the kitchen table, certain her parents would never want to sell.

That evening her dad called to her. "What's this?" he asked, holding up the card.

She explained, expecting him to chuckle and toss it away. Instead he stared at it thoughtfully before slipping it inside a shirt pocket. Kellie wondered why he cared, but nothing more was said about it that night.

Two days later her dad called a family meeting after dinner. When everyone was gathered, he started pacing, hands clasped behind his back.

"Your mother and I have decided to sell the house," he said, looking Kellie and Tommy squarely in the eyes.

Kellie sat there numb, too shocked to say anything. Tommy shrugged. "It doesn't matter to me," he said. "My buddy Jim and I found a place. We're moving in next month."

"Yes, well," Dad continued, "that's fine, but I want it clear to both of you that this was simply the right time to sell. Home prices are up, and Mom and I are getting closer to retirement. We want something smaller. We're considering buying something at the lake where some coworkers moved last year. That way we can fish and boat right in our own front yard."

Kellie finally found her voice. "A lake? There's no lake around here. Where are you talking about?"

Mom looked sympathetic. "It's not around here," she said quietly. "It's out in the country, near Malibu. It's really beautiful. I'm sure you'll love it."

"But . . . my whole life is here. You want me to leave it all behind? I don't want to move!"

Mom looked at her husband but didn't answer.

Dad cleared his throat. "Get used to the idea, Kellie," he said. "We've already signed the contract."

A sickening wave of adrenaline hit, making her head spin and her heart do flip-flops as the facts sank in: They were moving far away, too far to attend her present high school or be on the drill team. After months of effort and an all-too-brief taste of success, her parents were taking it all away.

Kellie deliberately did little to make the house look inviting whenever potential buyers came to look. Even so, a family bought it within a few weeks. Before summer was over, Tommy had moved to an apartment, and Kellie and her parents had settled into their new lakeside home.

Just as her parents had hoped, the new place was smaller. The main house sat way back from the lake on a hillside in a cluster of old trees. It had two bedrooms, one bathroom, a large living room with an open stone fireplace, and a tiny, old-fashioned kitchen. Her parents took the larger bedroom and made the second a home office. Downstairs, a dark cement basement had a laundry area and room for the pool table and Dad's workbench.

That left just one possible place for Kellie: the round guesthouse perched on a cliff about 30 yards in front of the main house, overlooking the lake. It was pretty, with lots of shade trees, its own porch and sun-deck, and big windows all around that looked out on the surrounding mountains, other homes across the way, and the water below. But there wasn't a shower or heater; she'd have to bathe in the main house and make do with a space heater. She didn't mind those hardships too much. But at night she hated being so far away from her parents in the main house, con-nected only by a long stone walkway with only one dim light.

Now, after three nights of insomnia, Kellie was again lying wide awake in the dark, feeling very small and alone. She couldn't get used to the pitch darkness of the country; she was used to city lights. The sounds of coyotes, owls, and other nocturnal critters fright-ened her. Her sixteenth birthday was coming up, but she wasn't ready for this much independence.

In the morning she dragged herself into the house for breakfast. She mumbled hello to her dad, who was drinking coffee and reading the paper in the living room. She found her mom cooking in the kitchen. "Mornin'," she said, yawning.

"Still not sleeping?" Mom asked, shaking her head. "You've got to get over your fears; rest is too important."

Kellie nodded, wondering exactly how to go about not being afraid. She decided to change the subject.

"Mom, what am I going to do about school? You keep saying we'll talk about it later, but classes start in two weeks."

Her mom served up eggs and orange juice and joined her at the small table near the back door.

"I know. I've been working on it. Actually, I think I've come up with a plan if you're willing to make some sacrifices."

Kellie groaned. She'd already made so many. "What's the plan?" She forced a lukewarm smile.

Her mom explained they could probably get special permission from the local high school principal to allow her to attend her old school. The hard part would be the commute. She'd have to wake up extra early on school mornings to carpool with her mom to a drop-off point, then connect with a bus to school. After school, she'd repeat everything in reverse, adding a two-hour wait at the library until her mom finished work.

In addition to all that, she'd walk a mile back and forth to her brother's place once a week to be in town for Wednesday night practice. He didn't have an extra bed, so she'd have to camp out on his floor overnight. On Fridays she'd stay for the football game and then spend the night at her aunt Betty's house.

It was exhausting just to think about, let alone do. But Kellie agreed to try. A few days later the local principal gave his permission. The decision was made.

Chapter 8

The
Parade

As the fall unfolded, everything seemed to go like clockwork. Sixteen-year-old Kellie was tired a lot and rarely saw Mary anymore, since they had different classes and were on different drill team squads. But Kellie grew used to the commuting and loved all the girls on her squad. She especially looked forward to practices and the fun of game night. Then one cold and windy Friday night in December, the night before the Santa Claus Lane Parade in Hollywood, everything stopped.

It happened right after the band, drill team, and football players had arrived in buses at the other team's field for an away game. Kellie came bounding down the steps of the bus just in time for Shawn, a football player from her school, to wave at her. His friendly gesture was such a surprise that she missed the last step and twisted her ankle.

Now, instead of performing in the halftime show

with her teammates on the field, she had to sit in the bleachers.

"Here." Miss Wang gently put ice on her swelling ankle. "This should help, but you're out for the night, maybe even for the parade."

Kellie's head shot up. "But my family's going to watch us on television! I have to be in it!"

Miss Wang shrugged, offering a sympathetic smile. "There's nothing I can do. Either you'll heal in time or you won't."

Bored and miserable, Kellie was glad when the game ended. She could hardly wait to get to her aunt's house.

Miss Wang dropped her off. After the first knock Kellie could hear her aunt's dog, Mabel, whining from inside until the front door opened.

"Howdy!" Aunt Betty exclaimed, brushing stray hairs away from her lively blue eyes. "You're early. What happened to pizza with your friends?"

"I hurt my ankle, so I skipped it," she explained, limping past the excited Australian shepherd.

Aunt Betty shooed Mabel away. "Here, let's get you to the kitchen," she said. "I'll make hot tea, and you can tell me all about it." Aunt Betty believed hot tea could cure almost anything.

Kellie sat at the table and watched her favorite aunt bustle around the faded pink kitchen in a housecoat and slippers, graying hair pulled back with a stretchy headband. She was younger than Kellie's mom, but painful arthritis made her appear older than her years.

"How about applesauce with your tea? Or maybe

grapefruit with sugar? I have pink or yellow, very juicy."

"Applesauce," Kellie decided, feeling more hopeful already.

"Here are some crackers, too," she said, plopping down an entire box.

"Thanks, Aunt Betty."

"Sure thing, Princess. Now tell me what happened."

Kellie recalled the whole embarrassing mess, including a full description of how cute Shawn was. Ever since Aunt Betty had taught her to read in that very kitchen, she'd felt free to tell her anything. Kellie even laughed as she recalled her ungraceful landing and the looks on everyone's faces, especially the football players'.

"It was awful," she confessed. "I blushed . . . I almost cried. And Shawn never even asked if I was all right!"

"Don't fret. He probably thought it'd embarrass you. Or maybe he's shy in front of his teammates. It's not easy being a teenage boy."

Just then Uncle Winn came in for water and a friendly hello before returning to the den to watch television with his youngest son, Steven, and daughter, Susan. With his gentle manner and lanky build, Uncle Winn always reminded Kellie of Jimmy Stewart from *It's a Wonderful Life*.

Kellie sipped her tea and decided to face the real problem. "Miss Wang says I can't do the parade tomorrow night unless my ankle's healed by afternoon. Is that possible?"

"Finish eating; then we'll figure it out."

When the tea and food were gone, Aunt Betty helped her into bed before perching on the edge of the blanket. "Here's what we'll do," she said. "First, I'll get a pillow to elevate your foot, and I'll wrap it in an Ace bandage. That keeps blood from filling the injury. You'll need a heating pad and an ice bag, which we'll alternate every 30 minutes or so, and aspirin for pain. Want something to read?"

"Sure, thanks . . . but about the ice; do we stop changing it when we go to sleep?"

"I'll set my alarm and bring fresh ice every two hours. When you feel it melt, switch to the heating pad. That should get the swelling down by tomorrow. You just have to have faith, that's all."

Kellie gulped, amazed at what Aunt Betty was willing to do. Her own parents had always left her alone to nurse herself through every illness, even chicken pox. Tears stung her eyes as she reached for a hug, sinking into the warm folds of her aunt's ample girth.

"Aunt Betty, you believe in God, right? I mean, you and Uncle Winn go to church on Sundays, and you say grace every Thanksgiving, right?"

"Yes, I've believed in God my whole life," she answered quietly. "Why?"

"Well, Mom doesn't. Neither does Dad." She pulled away and looked earnestly into her aunt's gentle face. "How come *you* go to church and Mom doesn't? I mean, you grew up together! Are you sure God's real? Do you pray to Him?"

"Mercy, Maude!" Aunt Betty exclaimed, standing. "Such big questions. Let me get the stuff. Then we'll sit right here and sort it all out."

That night Kellie asked questions about faith that she'd held in for years. Not every answer made perfect sense, but Betty patiently kept at it until Kellie started to believe there might really be a God in heaven.

After a long night, Kellie continued heating and icing her ankle the next day, reading magazines while the rest of the family went about their business. From her bed she heard her cousins talk and laugh respectfully with their folks. Each time, Aunt Betty and Uncle Winn responded with unhurried love and kindness.

It made Kellie envious. She wondered why her own parents were so different, so cranky and busy all the time. Too busy.

But by 3:00 her ankle felt so well that she forgot to be envious. Aunt Betty's faith had worked. Kellie was going to the parade!

When she marched down Hollywood Boulevard that night and performed for the welcoming crowds, she felt grateful for her aunt's tireless nursing and was glad they'd talked about God. She couldn't wait to tell Mom all about it!

Chapter 9

New
Friends

The next day Kellie talked all the way home. "It was so great, Mom," she enthused. "There were celebrities and floats and television cameras and reporters. And so many people!"

"I know!" Mom smiled. "We saw you on TV. You guys did a super job."

"Thanks! The weather was *so* cold, but it felt warmer once we started marching. My ankle didn't hurt much until the very end. I'll rest it tonight."

"Kellie, you had a wonderful experience, and I'm glad. But I'm afraid this will be your last year in drill team."

Kellie caught her breath. "But . . . why? I love it!"

Her mom nodded, never taking her eyes from the road. "I know, but all this commuting back and forth and spending the night at your brother's . . . well, it just isn't good for you. Dad and I have decided it's better if you transfer next year to the high school near the house."

For several miles Kellie tearfully pleaded her case, but nothing worked.

That night she sat on the cold, hard guesthouse steps staring out at the moonlit water, thinking of the friends she'd made in drill team and the fun she'd had performing. Without weekends at Aunt Betty's she'd lose the one person she had to talk to about friends, boys, and God. She would miss it all so much. Bitter sobs came, washing away her confidence and faith in a steady flow of tears.

When they subsided, she felt a surge of anger aimed directly at the beautiful lake below. Unable to stand the sight, she hid behind clenched hands. But the sound of bullfrogs wouldn't let her forget where she was or what living there had cost her. Realizing she was helpless to change the facts, she went inside for the night.

By midspring Kellie's harsh schedule had finally caught up with her. She came down with mono, a severe flulike illness that took weeks to recover from. Luckily, drill team had finished for the year. It was comforting to know that before she got sick she'd done her part to help them win first place in the city-wide competition.

As she recuperated at home, the thought of changing to a closer campus and getting up later on school mornings grew more appealing. But she worried about making all new friends her senior year.

More than ever, she resented moving there in the first place.

—

"Hand me your plate," Dad said.

Kellie obeyed, getting up from her dock chair. It was a warm June evening, just before sunset. A mother duck swam near the reeds, a string of quacking ducklings following behind. Kellie's mom was pulling sodas from an ice-filled cooler.

"Just a little," Kellie told him. He was piling her plate high with salad and other picnic foods.

She normally loved picnics, but this evening, nerves dulled her appetite. The lake community was hosting a dock party, during which neighbors spent hours boating from dock to dock, eating and drinking along the way. Kellie was over her mono, and felt well enough. She just wasn't interested in meeting the neighbors. So she took her food and settled moodily back into the chair, waiting for a chance to excuse herself and escape to her room.

"Hello the dock!" a voice called out.

An older man with gray hair and glasses approached in a weathered canoe. He was a stranger to her. She mumbled a hello and continued eating.

The man tied his boat and climbed onto the dock. He shook hands with her dad, said hello to her mom, and then came straight over to Kellie.

"Hi there," he said, offering a smile and a handshake. "I'm Ben Moore . . . I work with your dad. I understand you're transferring to our local high school next year."

She nodded, wondering why he was telling her all that.

"Well, I happen to know another family that just moved in across the lake. They have a girl your age who's transferring there too. I thought maybe you'd like to come with me now and meet her." His smile grew as he beamed at his own suggestion.

Kellie knew he wanted her to be excited at the news, but it only terrified her. She turned pleading eyes to her dad, hoping to wiggle out of this crazy suggestion. To her horror, he was beaming too. "That's a great idea, just what she needs," Dad agreed.

"Wonderful!" Ben said, eyes dancing with excitement. "Come on, let's go." He made a sweeping gesture toward his canoe.

Kellie looked from one parent to the other, wondering why they were doing this. She felt trapped, like a worm on a hook.

"Mom, I'm getting a headache. I was going to eat and then go to bed."

"Nonsense," Ben interrupted. "A canoe ride is the best thing for a headache. Fresh air!" Without waiting for more protests, he set her plate aside and gallantly took her hand.

"But I don't think . . . " she tried to argue. Before she could say any more, they were aboard the boat and gliding swiftly away from the safety of her dock.

Minutes later they landed at another dock. Behind it a manicured lawn led to a modern one-story ranch house. Ben introduced her to the older couple who lived there. "I thought maybe she could meet your daughter, Sara," he explained.

Not Alone

The woman nodded warmly. "Come," she invited. "I'll take you to her."

Kellie followed her inside to a back bedroom where a pretty teenage girl with dark shoulder-length hair and brown eyes sat on the floor listening to music and polishing her nails. Kellie could tell they were about the same height, but the other girl had a more grown-up figure.

"Sara," the woman said.

The girl looked up and smiled when she saw Kellie. In the blink of an eye, all worries evaporated. The girls clicked instantly. Before the evening ended, Sara invited her to return the next morning.

All that next day they talked about their old schools and compared them to the new one, tried on goofy outfits, and did each other's hair. In the afternoon they swam in the lake.

When it got late, Sara asked her to walk with her to another neighbor's house, the Fosters', to retrieve a forgotten beach towel from the day before. Their rambling two-story wood-and-stone house overflowed with teenagers, some who lived there and others who were just hanging out. Kellie shyly met each one, but was shocked to see most of them either drinking beer or smoking cigarettes, or both. Mr. and Mrs. Foster were there too, and seemed unconcerned. Kellie was glad when Sara announced they couldn't stay.

Walking back, Kellie mentioned the Fosters' relaxed attitude, hoping Sara wouldn't think she was uncool. "I know!" she agreed. "I mean, I'll have a beer or a smoke at parties, but my folks would flip if they ever knew."

"Yeah, mine too," Kellie agreed, secretly wondering if they really would. After all, Dad used to smoke, and Tommy had now taken up the habit. A sudden gust of hot wind blew across the road, scattering leaves and dust. She could feel her world shifting once again, this time in a whole new and dangerous direction.

Chapter 10

Ghost Stories

"H ey, you want to go see Mitch Hollis at his house?" Sara asked. She was rooting through a small wooden jewelry box, choosing which silver earrings to wear with her yellow halter top and jeans. "It's a really cool place." Sara waited for Kellie's answer, then shot her a questioning look. "Well, do you?"

It'd been several days since the girls had met during the dock party. They'd spent most of that time together. It was natural now for them to widen their circle of friends.

Kellie twisted a lock of hair, slowly meeting her gaze. "Which one is Mitch?"

Sara threw back her head and laughed. "He's the *really cute* guy I introduced you to in the Fosters' driveway. Don't tell me you don't remember . . . light- brown hair . . . great eyes . . . ring a bell?"

Kellie nodded and turned to hide her blush. "Are

you sure he won't mind us just showing up?"

Sara plopped brown and black feather earrings in Kellie's hand. "I already called him before you got here. He said to come over whenever. Now put these on. They go perfectly with the top you're wearing."

Unlike Kellie, Sara already had her driver's license and a sporty red car. It took only minutes to drive up and around the mountainside to where Mitch lived.

Along the way Sara explained the history of his house. "A long time ago, it belonged to Clark Gable . . . you know, the movie star? He used it as his hunting lodge. After Clark, some television producer bought it, then someone else, and now it belongs to Mitch and his mom and sister."

"How cool! Is it nice?"

"It's not fancy, but I like it. And . . ." She paused for effect. "It's *haunted*."

Kellie's eyes lit up with surprise. Then she laughed. "You're kidding, right? It's not *really* haunted!"

Sara slowed down for a sharp curve that overlooked the *M★A★S★H.* television film set. She then sped back up until they passed between two large stone pillars. She parked at the end of a long driveway and gave Kellie a challenging smile. "You can believe what you want, but I'm telling you it's haunted. I've seen it with my own eyes."

Kellie took a moment to study the enormous two-story wood-shingled structure. It loomed before her, nestled in the side of the mountain, its peaked roof lines piercing the crisp blue sky. Wide stone steps led one flight up to a generous, covered veranda and front door. Large picture windows ran along the front and side of the house to take advantage of the mountain views. A patchy lawn grew in front; a weathered barn sat at the back. A tall wood fence covered with roses and magenta bougainvilleas surrounded the property. It was old and needed repairs, but was by far the biggest, grandest house she'd ever seen.

Kellie followed Sara up the steps, pausing briefly to pet a sleepy Saint Bernard. "What's down there?" Kellie pointed to the home's first story.

"They turned that into a separate apartment. It has another entrance in back. I think some guy rents it."

Peeking through the ornate screen door, Kellie thought about the old black-and-white "haunted house" movies she used to watch as a kid and the "ghost story" books she'd read late at night under the covers by flashlight. If *this* house really was haunted, it would bring all those pretend stories to life.

Sara knocked. A male voice called from the back of the house, telling them to come in.

Kellie was so focused on the "ghost" that she forgot to worry about Mitch. Leaving shyness behind, she stepped boldly inside the living room, taking in its scuffed wood floors, knotty pine walls, and heavy stone fireplace. When her eyes adjusted to the dim lighting, she found herself staring at her own reflection in a floor-to-ceiling framed mirror hanging opposite the front door. She quickly turned away, determined to deal with Sara's claim head-on.

"So where's the ghost?" she asked sarcastically.

Sara's only answer was a short laugh at her friend's disbelief. They were alone in the living room. Mitch was still in another part of the house.

Kellie turned in a slow circle, looking for anything out of the ordinary. "OK, where are you?" she called out, her voice louder than normal. "Come on. If you're real, show yourself!"

A long stretch of silence fell as they stood stock-still, waiting to see what might happen. Nothing in the room moved until Mitch emerged from a back hallway, startling them both. "Hey," he said, flashing a somewhat shy smile. "What are you guys doing out here? It sounded like you were yelling at someone."

In that instant Kellie's own shyness came flooding back. How could she explain?

Luckily, Sara spoke up first. "Don't mind her," she giggled, rolling her eyes in mock horror. "Kellie has this thing for ghosts, and I just got done telling her about yours. So she was trying to make him put in an appearance."

Mitch fixed his gaze on Kellie. "So you believe in ghosts? That's good, 'cause we've got one, all right." He turned to Sara. "Tell her what happened the last time you were here."

"A bunch of us were in the kitchen when the cupboard door opened by itself; the dishes inside started rattling and moving."

Kellie wanted to believe her, but couldn't. "Have you ever heard of earthquakes? You can do better than that."

"I'm telling you, it happened!" Sara insisted. "Besides, *nothing* else in the kitchen moved. It was freaky. And you should have seen the cat! Her fur stuck straight out like a porcupine's. Poor Pumpkin— she yowled and took off running."

"OK, maybe this place *is* haunted. Can I see the rest?"

"Sure, follow me," he said, leading the way.

It was a fun visit. Having Sara there made it easier for Kellie to get to know Mitch, something she'd secretly wanted all along. Even so, it was hard to get her mind off the ghost. She wanted so much to see or hear him. But to her disappointment, nothing unusual happened there that day.

Chapter 11

Spooky Summer

The next week Sara and Kellie signed up for an easy summer school class so they could get used to their new campus. After school they drove to the beach or swam in the lake. As they got to know more people, they went to more parties at which the guests drank beer and smoked pot. Kellie knew it was wrong and worried about getting caught. But she did nothing to stop herself. She liked being accepted by the lake crowd. It was a new life.

"This house is pretty old, isn't it?" Sara asked.

The girls had finished their summer school homework. Now they were drinking sodas and sunbathing on the guesthouse sundeck in shorts and bathing suit tops. They watched an older couple putt around in an electric boat, enjoying the day.

Kellie liked watching the sailboats, too, but there

were none today. The wind was too calm for sailing. "Yeah. I think it's almost 100 years old," she answered.

"So whoever lived here first *must* be dead already. Hey, I have a great idea! If you have a Ouija board, we could try contacting them."

They ran inside—Kellie to the closet to pull out the dusty board game, Sara to make room on the messy floor for them to play. The neighbors' gray-and-black German shepherd, Batika, followed them inside and curled up for a nap.

Getting comfortable, they both placed several fingers on the wooden pointer positioned in the middle of the board. At first, nothing happened. Then slowly the pointer began moving around to different letters.

"Are you making it move?" Kellie accused.

"No!"

Sara spelled the letters out; it was a man's name. The "spirit" then used more letters and numbers to tell them he'd lived in the guesthouse many decades before and was now haunting it. After that, the pointer moved faster as the "ghost" communicated more information, hooking them in as their curiosity grew.

While they were still playing the game, the plant hanging above them began swaying in circles. Kellie looked outside; there still was no breeze. Before that mystery could be solved, the radio they'd been listening to turned off, then back on again.

The girls shared glances, but chose to go on playing until Batika got their attention. The large dog was fearless when facing natural enemies, such as raccoons or potential intruders. Now she awoke from her nap with a start, looking around the room with eyes wide with fear.

"It's all right, girl," Kellie soothed. The dog rushed to her side, whimpering and trembling.

"She sees something and it's scaring her," Sara warned. Then she pushed the pointer away. "I'm done. I don't want to play this anymore."

Kellie agreed that the game had gone too far, producing scarier results than either of them was ready for. But as the summer unfolded, they pushed those initial fears aside and dared to play again and again, unable to resist the lure of the occult.

When fall arrived, the girls officially registered as seniors. Kellie had earned her driver's license by then, but didn't own a car, so she rode to school with Sara. To their delight, they discovered the school had an open policy. With no fences or gates around the campus, students were free to come and go at lunchtime without restriction. Giddy with freedom, the girls sometimes failed to come back for afternoon classes. Eventually they started skipping school altogether and went to the beach instead, feeling less guilty every time. As the truancies added up, Kellie's grades fell. She solved the problem by hiding her report cards and pulling truancy notices from the mail before her folks could see them.

Along with cutting class, partying was becoming a regular habit. That only made it harder for Kellie to feel like going to school. When she did go, her mind was often fuzzy and tired from hangovers.

Schoolwork and high grades had always come easy to her. Now just showing up was a burden.

In the meantime, she noticed that things were getting strange at the guesthouse. She couldn't tell if it was the beer and pot or the Ouija board or both. Either way, she'd opened herself up to a whole new realm of the spirit world.

At first it was little things.

House keys would come up missing from her purse. Each time she'd carefully empty it, even shake out the lining, and find nothing. Then later, when she'd be in another part of town, the keys would suddenly reappear at the top of that same purse. After it happened a few times, Kellie's parents got exasperated and accused her of being irresponsible. Before she could prove them wrong, a basket of dirty clothes went missing for days, then showed up in the basement. No one seemed to know how it had gotten there. Other things got moved around or lost in the guesthouse, making her doubt her own memory at times.

Eventually Kellie came to feel pretty sure that all these weird happenings could be blamed on the "ghost," but her suspicions were confirmed when she finally met him face to face. It happened one morning when she was late getting up for school. To her surprise, the "ghost" woke her up with a tap on the shoulder, offering a smile and a helping hand out of bed. As soon as her feet hit the floor, he vanished.

Even though she couldn't always see the "ghost," she knew he was there. Just like the first time she'd brought out the Ouija board, he now played similar tricks all the time, turning the lights, radio, and television set off and on with alarming frequency.

At first, all that attention made her feel special, almost like having a roommate of sorts. Like Mitch, she now had her very own real-life "ghost." But those feelings wavered when other strange "spirits" began interrupting her sleep to fight what seemed like pointless battles, their only possible purpose to frighten her into powerless submission.

Each time she would find herself caught in a dreamlike state, completely paralyzed and unable to speak. Like someone drowning, she'd fight to move and breathe as the walls and windows of the guesthouse seemed to fly at her and recede again and again while she wrestled with someone she couldn't see. The battle would last until the spell broke on its own, and she'd suddenly come fully awake, breathless and terrified.

One night Kellie asked Sara to sleep over, hoping her friend might keep her safe. The attack came anyway. In fact, at one point, it looked as if Sara herself were involved, even pinning Kellie down as she fought for control. But when the spell broke, Kellie looked over and saw Sara sleeping peacefully beside her, unaware. *What was happening to her?* she wondered. *How had her innocent "ghostly fun" gotten so far out of hand?*

"Turn that song up; it's my favorite!" Kellie urged. She was ironing her jeans in the basement while Sara kept her company.

"OK," Sara obliged. "Hey, I need a bathroom. Are your parents asleep?"

"Yeah; you'll have to go out to the guesthouse."

It was already dark, but Sara went without complaining. Minutes later she ran back into the basement breathless, her wraparound skirt flying, face pale and eyes looking panicky. "You'll never guess what happened to me out there!"

She described how she'd heard fingers drumming loudly on the television set right outside the bathroom door, as if someone were irritated and impatient for her to get done and leave.

"When I came out, there was nobody there!" she cried. "That ghost of yours was trying to get rid of me! I am *never* going in there by myself again!"

In that moment Kellie stopped feeling special and began feeling trapped instead. The "ghost" apparently wanted her all to himself.

Chapter 12

Party
Pressures

Hand me one of those beers," someone said.

Kellie looked up. It was Kent, a tall, thin boy she didn't know very well. It was a cool spring evening, and a few of the local kids had thrown a party on the clubhouse lawn. One of them had invited Kent, who lived in the next town.

"Come on, I'm thirsty," he urged.

She stopped eating and leaned to grab a cold can from the ice-filled cooler under the picnic table by her feet. He swayed as he accepted it without thanks, tossing away a cigarette to push pale, limp hair from his bleary eyes. His T-shirt was grungy, his jeans torn. The laces of one sneaker were untied, inviting disaster.

"Maybe you should slow down on those," she cautioned.

"Nah," he laughed. "I'm just gettin' started."

She watched him stagger away before taking another bite of cake.

Not Alone

Out of the darkness Mitch and Sara emerged from a group of laughing teens and came over to Kellie's picnic table. "Stop eating and come with us," Mitch invited, resting smiling eyes on her. "We're taking a ~~rowboat~~ to the dam." He looked especially handsome in new jeans and a long-sleeved shirt.

"What for?" She was on her second slice and wasn't full yet.

Sara whisked the half-eaten dessert into the garbage before Kellie could stop her. "I can't understand why you never get fat!" she complained. "Now come on, before someone else takes the boat. It'll be fun!"

The two girls climbed aboard the empty boat while Mitch grabbed the wooden oars. He was about to shove off when Kent came loping across the community dock and jumped in with them, nearly losing his shoe, setting the boat rocking wildly in the ink-like water.

"Hey!" Mitch warned. "Watch it! I'm not in the mood for a swim."

"Sorry," the boy apologized. But his self-satisfied grin said otherwise. "Hey, this is cool. Goin' for a boat ride!"

Kellie rolled her eyes and turned to watch a second boatload of teens take off at the same time. Like train cars on parallel tracks, the two vessels moved together across the still, moonlit lake.

Mitch rowed with smooth, rhythmic motions, creating a soothing sound as the oars sliced again and again through water, propelling them past private docks and the big island, then crossing the main part of the lake. The moon gave an eerie glow to several silvery clouds overhead, while in the distance a flurry of ducks squawked and complained. It was a peaceful night . . . until all the beer Kent had consumed suddenly kicked in.

As Kellie looked on, the tall teen slowly, slowly, like a tree being felled in the forest, began toppling over sideways. With nothing to stop him, he kept going until his head hit the water, half submerged, like a fish on the line.

Everyone seemed to move at once. Mitch heard Kent's gurgles and craned his own head around to see what was happening. Sara and Kellie leaped from their seats and frantically grabbed one arm each.

"Pull him up!" Mitch ordered. "He must have passed out. He'll drown like that!"

The girls tugged with all their might, but Kent was too heavy. In his unconscious state, he wasn't using his own muscles to help; he was nearly dead-weight.

"We can't lift him," Sara cried. "We need help!"

Mitch carefully, swiftly pulled the oars into the boat so they wouldn't be lost in the water. Then he leaned one arm way back and grabbed the back of Kent's shirt. With a mighty tug, together they pulled him out of the water.

As he came upright, Kent sputtered and coughed, then shook his head as his eyes fluttered open. He looked at the others in total confusion. "Hey," he complained, pointing at his shirt. "I'm all wet!"

Mitch shook his head in disgust. "OK, one of you sit next to this guy so he stays out of trouble," he ordered.

Not Alone

Sara was stronger, so she stayed beside Kent while Kellie moved to the end of the boat to keep it balanced. He swayed a couple more times, but Sara's firm hold kept him in the boat.

By the time they reached the dam, Kent was wide awake. Shaking off Sara's helping hand, he grabbed some rebar sticking out of the cement and tied up the boat before climbing out.

"Careful!" Sara warned.

"I got it!" Kent answered belligerently.

The others got out too, but with more care. In a single file they walked to the end of the dam and clambered onto a boulder, then along the side of the hill facing the back side of the dam. They kept going until they found a good spot to sit. From there they could see the entire dam from top to bottom, all the way down to where lake water spilled into a creek nearly 100 feet below.

Kellie scanned the area to locate the other teens. She could see them tying up at a dock near the dam, laughing and talking. She was about to wave them over when she realized Kent was not on his way to join either group. He was still at the dam, alone.

"Look!" she cried, pointing in his direction. He'd stepped off firm ground and was staggering across the narrow ledge of the dam wall like a drunken tightrope walker. Each step made his arms flail wildly as the rest of his body struggled to maintain balance.

"Oh!" Sara screamed. "I can't look!"

At that moment, about midway across the dam, Kent lost his balance and fell. By some miracle he landed on top of the wall flat on his back, one arm and leg in the water and the other set dangling over the side with little to keep him from falling to his death.

"Man!" It was Mitch, grumbling as he rushed back to the dam. "I guess it's up to me to take him back before he kills himself! You guys go with the others. I'll see you at the clubhouse."

Kellie sat motionless for a time, watching Kent flail helplessly atop the dam until Mitch rescued him. He looked like the world's worst fool. In that moment she realized it wasn't his lack of intelligence that had nearly ended his life. It was the beer and the pot he'd happily, foolishly consumed all evening that had put him in harm's way.

Then her thoughts turned back to last month, when she'd learned that another boy at another party had taken too many pills before going for a swim by himself in the lake. Someone had found him the next morning, still in the lake. He'd drowned.

All at once, partying didn't seem like much fun anymore.

Chapter 13

Beaver Lake

For the rest of that spring Kellie and Sara struggled to keep their grades high enough to finish high school. Sometimes it looked doubtful, and more than one teacher said it was hopeless. They'd missed too much school, making both sets of parents angry. With only three weeks left in the school year, the girls flew into panic mode and begged their teachers for makeup work. The last-ditch effort was barely enough to allow them to graduate with their class in June.

It was great to be done at last. Kellie welcomed summer with relief. She just wished she had more to do than party. Her only real fun came when a film crew used Sara's house to make a movie with John Travolta. But that didn't last long.

In fact, as the summer dragged slowly by, the future began looking less and less promising. She hadn't applied to any colleges or universities. She didn't have a job. She'd completely wasted the last year goofing off while friends suffered one mishap after another, including jailtime and car accidents.

Now it was Labor Day weekend, her eighteenth birthday, and she'd decided to join three friends her own age who belonged to Alcoholics Anonymous for a campout in Utah. Kellie borrowed her mom's station wagon, picked up Christine, Bob, and Kevin, and drove to Beaver Lake. No one brought fishing gear, but Kevin did bring his rifle for target practice. At the campsite the girls took one cabin, the boys another.

In the morning they ate breakfast and planned their day.

"Let's go swimming," Kellie suggested.

Christine wrinkled her nose. "The water's too cold," she countered.

"But the weather's hot."

The boys exchanged looks.

"I'm with Christine," Bob said. "The lake's too cold. I say we go hiking."

"So hike," Kellie announced. "I'm going swimming."

"Suit yourself," Kevin shrugged, focused on covering his fair, freckled skin with plenty of sunscreen.

They dropped Kellie off at the lake. She showed them where she'd be swimming and watched them drive away.

She spread a towel atop a flat boulder overlooking the water. Not another soul in sight. Pushing fear away, she walked to the edge, inhaled deeply, held her breath, and leaped gracefully outward. Her dive was perfect, but when she plunged beneath the sparkling surface, she got the shock of her life. Instead of warm water like she was used to at home, this was icy—like melted snow. The cold pierced her like tiny knives, cramping her muscles and stiffening her limbs as she inched slowly upward.

Breaking the surface, she gasped for air, but her lungs wouldn't expand. The frigid water constricted her chest and restricted her breathing. Her heart felt ready to burst. In a panic she tried to yell for help, but could only whisper.

She struggled to keep her head above water long enough to take in air while looking for an escape. The boulder's sheer, high face wouldn't let her climb out. The nearest shoreline was nearly 25 feet away. Kellie was a strong swimmer, but the cold kept her from treading water. She started to sink. She'd been in danger before, but this was the first time she thought she might actually die.

Looking up, her terror-filled eyes pierced the heavens, seeking the unknown. "God," she whispered, "if You're real, don't let me die! Please help me!"

Immediately an illogical hope pushed her to try swimming . . . again. Slowly her limbs moved doggie style, inching forward like a crawling infant's. Every few seconds she gulped more air, ignoring the burn in her lungs. All the while, she silently begged God not to let her drown.

After what seemed like an eternity her feet touched bottom. From there she crawled, exhausted, onto wet sand and lay shivering like a wounded animal until she could make it back to the boulder, where she gratefully stretched out on her towel and baked in the warm sun, pondering if God had just saved her life.

The next day all four teens returned to the lake for a hike and some target practice. They had no plans to swim.

Suddenly Bob whooped with excitement. "Look!" He pointed to a clump of trees. "A rowboat, with oars and everything! Let's see if it floats."

They ran to inspect it and found it "seaworthy." The boys immediately launched it.

"You girls go first," Kevin suggested. "Then we'll go."

Kellie was leery, but couldn't resist the adventure. She climbed in and grabbed the oars while Christine settled at the other end. Soon they were gliding across open water.

About 70 yards out they made a wide turn back. Her arms tired from the exercise, Kellie set the oars down and looked toward the shoreline. Kevin's rifle was clearly upraised and pointed in their direction. At that moment a whistling sound whizzed past her ear.

"What was *that*?" she yelped.

Christine's face was ashen. "I think they're shooting at us!"

Kellie whirled back and waved frantically. "Hey! You're going to *hit* us! Stop shooting!"

But the whistling continued, bullets flying closer and closer, slicing the water nearby. The girls kept yelling and waving, expecting injury or death any second.

For the second time in as many days, Kellie pleaded with God for her life. "Please," she begged softly. "Make it stop."

And just like that, it did. She smiled at Christine in relieved disbelief. Her friend wasn't smiling. "They could've killed us!" she sobbed. "And look! They shot the boat!"

Sure enough, a walnut-sized hole was letting in dark, icy water. Kellie knew from her near-disaster the day before that they could never swim safely all the way back to shore from this far out; they *had* to get closer to land.

"Here, Christine, take the oars. You row while I scoop!"

Christine rowed hard while Kellie used her hands, then her shoes, to bail out the water. It was a losing battle, but they somehow got to shore before it sank all the way. "What's wrong with you?" Christine yelled at the guilt-stricken boys. "Why were you shooting at us?"

"We thought we were shooting *near* you," Kevin stammered.

"Yeah," Bob chimed in. "We just wanted to scare you a little."

"*Now* what?" Kellie demanded. "You've wrecked someone's boat! We'll have to find the owners and tell them."

"Hey, *I* can't pay for a new boat," Kevin said. "I say we leave town, *now*." He looked to Bob for support, who nodded agreement.

Christine shrugged in resignation. "Maybe they're right," she said. "We should probably just get out of here."

This time Kellie was sure God had saved her life. She owed Him *something*. She wanted to do the right thing. But she felt helpless to resist her friends, so they ran to the cabins to pack while rumors flew through the campground of angry men with shotguns looking for whoever had ruined their boat. It was a long, frantic drive back to Los Angeles, but they made it without being followed.

Dropping her friends off, Kellie bid them goodbye and drove home. It was late when she pulled into the driveway. Her parents would be asleep, so she went straight to the guesthouse. She set everything down and slid the key into the lock. It stubbornly refused to turn, keeping her out. As an owl hooted in a tree behind her, she saw the door curtain slowly move to the side, as if someone were looking out to see who was there.

"It's only me," she quipped, easing her jitters while appeasing the shy "ghost."

The key immediately turned, and the old door swung open. Sighing, she made herself go inside. More than ever, she hated being there alone, especially at night. But where else could she go? Too tired to unpack, she crawled into bed and slept.

Chapter 14

Stepping Out

You'll do as I tell you!" Dad slammed his beer down on the end table. His dark eyes stared furiously at Kellie across the room.

"You're not being fair!" she accused. "I'm 18! I should be able to do what I want."

He tried to stand, but wobbled on the way up. "Look," he growled. "*I* say what goes on around here, no matter how old you are. So you will do the jobs I tell you to do and come home at a decent hour. Understand?"

Kellie felt angry sobs threatening to erupt. She spun on her heels and fled before a single tear fell. But in the guesthouse a torrent soaked the pillow as she thought about what to do. Why couldn't he talk to her the way Uncle Winn spoke to Steven and Susan? Why did her dad have to be so mean about everything?

She needed to get away, to make her own decisions, to live her own life. Ellen had invited her to come live with them and go to college. But she didn't want to move that far away from all her friends. After a while she mopped her face and sat up. She'd made up her mind. She would move out, but she'd do it her own way . . . soon.

Over the next few days Kellie and her mom came up with a plan. Kellie found a room to rent not far from their old house. Her mom gave her a small loan and lined up a part-time library job for Kellie at the downtown community college where she worked. They would carpool together.

On moving day Mitch brought a pickup truck and helped Kellie load up her belongings while her dad watched from inside with a stony expression. He said nothing until they carried her bulky mattress down the long walkway; then he rushed outside. For a moment Kellie thought he might offer to help. He didn't. "Where do you think you're taking that?" he bellowed.

"Dad, I need a bed," Kellie said cautiously. "It is *my* bed."

"Yeah? Well, *I* bought it! Put it back."

Just then her mom rushed out to join them. "Fweedy," she soothed, using his pet name. "We don't need an extra mattress. Let her take it."

He glared at the group and let out a grunt. "Ah, take it. You always do what you want anyway."

Kellie watched him stomp back inside. She could breathe again, but her heart felt bruised.

"Is this it?" her mom asked.

"Yeah," Kellie answered. "I just have to lock up."

"Never mind," she said, waving them away. "I'll do that. You guys go before something else happens."

That night Kellie unpacked and arranged her new room. It was small, but it had its own bathroom. The kitchen and laundry room would be shared with the landlord, Mrs. Turner, and her 13-year-old son, Nick.

It felt strange living with people who would never spend time with her, but she took comfort knowing she could come and go as she pleased, with no one looking over her shoulder. When she closed her eyes to sleep, she hoped with all her heart she'd be happy here.

In no time Kellie adjusted to her new routine. Mornings she worked in the library's periodicals section. Afternoons she had class, including her favorite, art. Her friends lived too far away for partying, so she decided to give sobriety a try, hoping it would make school easier. So far, it was working.

As fall turned the weather colder and the days shorter, she kept herself busy. The frantic pace kept away the loneliness until one blustery Saturday night when the busyness ran out, leaving an unexpected void. Kellie found herself with nothing at all to do. Homework was done. She'd left her television at the guesthouse. The radio didn't help. She felt bored and very alone. She missed the lake crowd. She tried to amuse herself, to tune out the emptiness, but nothing worked.

She phoned Mitch. "Hey, what're you doing?" she asked.

"Not much. Mom's out of town, so some friends came over."

"I thought I'd take the bus to the lake market. Can you pick me up there?"

He agreed, but she immediately had second thoughts. She wanted to see everyone, but was afraid of losing her sobriety. It was probably a mistake. "OK," she blurted out. "I'll leave now."

Grabbing a coat, she ran to the bus stop. By the time she reached his house, it was full of teenagers, including his younger sister, Angie, a girl known for getting into trouble. Kellie hadn't spent much time with her before, but at 14, she looked like a grown-up hippie: feathers in her bleached-blond hair, multiple earrings, and heavy makeup. When Angie handed her a beer, they instantly became friends.

Later, when most of the kids had left, Kellie sat in front of the fire telling Mitch about her new place when she noticed something strange out of the corner of her eye. It was a beautiful young woman, smiling at her through the window. Instinctively Kellie smiled back, watching the woman turn and continue up the steps. That's when it hit her: for someone to look through that window, they'd have to be 10 feet tall, maybe more.

"Mitch, I think I just saw your ghost!"

He turned, but the woman had disappeared.

Kellie slept that night at Sara's house and tried to tell her about seeing Mitch's "ghost." But Sara only wanted to talk about her new job at the mall and plans to find an apartment. Her interests had grown far beyond the lake and the occult.

The next day they returned to Mitch's house to party a little more. When it got late, Sara drove Kellie home. "See you," Kellie called out, watching Sara drive away.

Inside, Mrs. Turner was waiting. Her usually neat, shoulder-length brown hair was limp and uncombed, her eyes worried.

"We had a problem while you were gone," she said.

"What happened?"

"Well, last night, we heard banging noises coming from your room. And then later, when Nick was asleep, I heard heavy footsteps in the hall outside my bedroom most of the night. That's never happened here before. Can you explain why it's happening now?"

Kellie's heart sank as she listened. This was just like at the lake. The "ghost" had followed her! In a rush of words she explained some of her past, trying not to scare the woman. She didn't want to be asked to leave. "I'm sure it'll stop now that I'm back," she promised.

"It had better." Mrs. Turner gave her a stern look and left the room.

Suddenly exhausted, Kellie wanted nothing but bed and sleep. But when she opened the door, a horrible sight met her. The entire bedroom was a shambles: pictures torn from the walls, books on the floor, jewelry strewn about, and the covers a tangled mess on the bed.

"Oh!" she cried, covering her mouth.

It took a long time to clean up. When everything was back in order, she flipped off the light and crawled into bed, closing her eyes to the dark. Despite her fears, drowsiness came quickly, pulling her toward sleep.

A pleasant dream formed in her mind like a favorite movie when suddenly loud, hideous laughter filled the room, jolting her awake. It sounded like the deep voice of a man, only harsher and more sarcastic than any man's laughter that she'd ever heard. As it continued, it grew louder and more intense, echoing off the walls.

Horrified, she lay stock-still, afraid to move or even open her mouth. There was nothing to do but wait for it to stop. She wanted to scream, but thoughts of Mrs. Turner's warning kept her silent. The laughter lasted about a minute before stopping abruptly, as if someone had pushed the mute button.

She stared into the darkness, trying to make sense of it all. There was only one explanation. The "ghost" had laughed at her for coming home high on beer and pot and for foolishly believing all those months that she'd left him behind in the guesthouse. Obviously she couldn't move away from the problem; there was no safe place for her anywhere. Even without her dad giving orders, her life wasn't her own after all.

Chapter 15

Home Again

The next day Mrs. Turner, to Kelli's surprise, said nothing about the hideous laughter. After that, fear drove Kellie to stay sober. Even so, the "ghost" was definitely back, causing problems that she tried to keep hidden. Despite those efforts, everything gradually unraveled like a torn blanket. The night battles resumed, making her too tired to function at work and forcing her to drop classes she didn't really need. At home she noticed that her landlord had fallen into the habit of talking to her only when necessary. When Mrs. Turner finally suggested that Kellie move out, it didn't surprise her. It was time.

Kellie found a modest rental to share with Christine. But money was scarce, and the "ghost" followed her there, too. When Christine moved back home after just a few weeks, Kellie decided to do the same. By spring she was back home, struggling to finish out the semester while the easy reach of old friends broke her down until sobriety went out the window.

Meanwhile, all the old "ghost" problems in the guesthouse remained, plus some new ones. The biggest hassle was her art; whenever she painted for class, an unseen hand would knock her off the little painter's stool or upset the canvas. In class the other students mentioned that some of the images in her work disturbed them, bringing down her confidence and tempting her to give up painting altogether. She longed to talk to a grown-up about it, but who'd believe her? And what could they do about it?

"Here, draw something." It was Amy, a girl who lived across the lake, near the Fosters'. She and Kellie were at Amy's house, listening to music. Amy brushed back her bangs and held out a pad of paper.

Kellie took the pad and quickly sketched a face, not bothering to fill in details. She handed it back and got comfortable in the window seat overlooking the lake.

Suddenly Amy gasped. "It moved!" she cried, pointing to the drawing. "Come see!"

Kellie rushed to look, but there was only the same face she'd drawn a minute before, and it wasn't moving. She nudged Amy playfully. "Seeing things?" she teased.

"No. It *did* move!"

Kellie laughed. Like most of her friends, Amy knew all about her "ghost."

"I guess I believe you. The ghost has been messing with my artwork lately. Sorry it scared you."

Not Alone

"Hey, that reminds me," Amy said, tossing the drawing away. "I saw you last Saturday night, in the guesthouse. You were on your bed drawing, with your stereo on full blast."

Kellie gave her a quizzical look. "How could you see me? You weren't there. You weren't even in town. You said you were visiting cousins in San Francisco."

"I know. I was doing astro projection . . . you know, mind travel. I could see you, but you couldn't see me. I do it all the time. It's fun!"

Kellie shook her head. "You're goofy. That's not even possible." She tapped her foot, thinking of a test. "What song was I listening to?"

" 'Stairway to Heaven.' You played it again and again. And you were drawing a *horse*."

A shiver ran down Kellie's spine. How could Amy know those things? Glancing out the window, she saw her small round guesthouse perched high on the distant cliff. It was too remote for anyone to spy on her. "Did you see anything else?"

Amy's expression filled with self-importance. "I saw something *really weird*. Two men—no, angels—I think—were fighting over you with swords. One was all in black, and his side of the house was dark. The other was all in white, and his side of the house was really bright. Like yin and yang, you know? That's why you couldn't go into the closet, because it was on the dark side. You started to go in a couple of times, remember? But then you changed your mind. Anyway, you looked scared, but I knew you couldn't see them fighting."

Kellie sighed with exasperation. She liked Amy, but her story was unbelievable! Except . . . she clearly remembered avoiding the closet, even though she'd needed some art pencils stored in there. And Amy had been right about the other stuff, too. But angels? They were just something on greeting cards!

"You're telling me you saw *real angels*, and they were *fighting*? Over *me*? That's crazy!"

Amy shrugged with a who-cares expression and began messing with one of the many rings on her fingers.

"I know what I saw."

"OK, forget the angels. What about this astro projection? Can you teach me how to do it?"

So Amy explained the basics.

"It's better if you take a class, though. A seminar's coming up. You should go."

That night Kellie tried to picture fighting angels. It was scarier than imagining the "ghost." Maybe if she went to the seminar, she'd be able to go places with astro projection, just like the spirits, and then they wouldn't scare her as much. It was worth a try.

Kellie sat cross-legged on the floor with dozens of other people in a hotel conference room. She was following the seminar trainer's instructions: eyes closed, mind focused, "visualizing" her spirit guide. This, the instructor promised, was the first step to learning astro projection.

For hours Kellie tried. But she only got a back-ache and the feeling that she was imagining more than visualizing . . . especially when her spirit guide started looking like a boy she once knew. By the time that first night ended, she was convinced that it was a waste of time.

When she talked to Amy the next day, she told her as much. "It was too hard!" she complained. "I really wanted to learn, but it didn't work."

"I know; it took me a long time to get it. Go back tonight and try again."

Kellie said no. She was done.

That afternoon she went to take a shower. She let Batika inside the main house for company, but made her stay in the hallway right outside the bathroom door. Kellie took her time getting everything ready, holding her fingers in the shower spray until it turned warm and steamy. Finally she cracked the bathroom window for air and could hear her dad talking and laughing outside with a neighbor.

And that's when it started . . . the sound of someone's fist pounding on the wall behind the shower, the wall that made up one side of her parents' bedroom. The pounding got harder and louder, making the shower doors rattle.

Outside, her father laughed again. And Mom was at the store. There was no one else in the house besides Kellie and Batika! Unable to stand it, she switched off the water. She was reaching for the bathroom door when the pounding suddenly stopped.

Still sitting in the hall, the dog looked up at her and trembled. "Batika, how are you, girl? Did you hear that? You did, didn't you?"

She rubbed her fur until they both calmed down.

Later, she asked her dad casually if he'd heard any noise coming from the house during his conversation in the driveway. He said he had not. When she got into bed that night, she lay there for hours, afraid to stay awake, but even more afraid to fall asleep. Had the seminar made things worse? Is that why the "ghost" had pounded at her so furiously? Maybe he was mad at her for trying to get help. It seemed that no matter what she did, the "ghost" problem always got worse, never better.

Chapter 16

Turning
Point

When the spring semester ended, Kellie took the summer off. No classes, no job. She needed time to figure things out, get her life back on track. Before things got too serious, though, she hit the beach.

"Can you hand me the tanning oil?" Kellie held out her hand.

"Here you go." Angie tossed it with a sassy smile.

Kellie caught it, thinking how much she'd grown to like the spunky teen.

The weather at Zuma Beach was a perfect 80 degrees. She and Angie spent the day bodysurfing and soaking up rays. When the late-afternoon sun turned the sky faintly pink and the ocean an intense aquamarine blue, the wind picked up too. It was time to go.

They headed for Angie's house, speeding through the narrow canyon as the sun sank below the mountains behind them. By the time they reached the lake, the unlit roads were very dark. Kellie slowed for each tight, twisting curve, winding past cabins and the lake store. They were passing the deserted park when something in the road caught her eye, making her scream.

"Did you see that?" she cried, swerving to miss it. "I hope it was only a *doll's* head!"

"I don't think it was," Angie whimpered. She twisted around to look out the back. "Hey, it's gone! Where'd it go?"

"I'll circle the park. It *has* to be there."

A minute later they were back where they'd started. She drove slowly, switching to high beams. The road was bare. Not even a fallen leaf disturbed the emptiness.

"I don't get it," Kellie whispered. "Could some-one have jumped from the bushes to grab it?"

"No, no one came out! I would've seen them."

"Let's get out of here." All at once Kellie under-stood what was happening, but still had trouble be-lieving her own eyes. The "ghost" had put a severed head in the middle of the road! She'd almost hit it, too. Maybe that was the idea . . . to force her into an accident. Her hands grew sweaty on the steering wheel, despite the cool night air. She glanced at Angie's frightened expression. They'd both seen it this time; there was no way for Kellie to pretend it hadn't really happened. This was too much. It had to stop!

She drove quickly to the house, and they ran in-side. She knew Mitch was spending the night at a friend's house. Their mom, Mrs. Hollis, was in the living room with her friend Ted.

"Mom," Angie burst out. "You won't believe what just happened!" She told her the whole story and waited.

Mrs. Hollis, a young-looking mom who often wore her daughter's clothes, turned to her friend and shrugged helplessly. "Any ideas, Ted?"

"I think I know what happened," he offered. "Have either of you experimented with the occult recently?" He was a big man with rosy cheeks and a thick head of hair. His eyes met Kellie's with a steady gaze, serious but full of kindness.

"Occult?" Kellie asked.

"Yeah. Contacting ghosts, using Ouija boards, going to fortunetellers. That sort of thing?"

"Yeah. How'd you know?"

"Because people don't usually experience what you did tonight unless they've invited it. I can show you how to make it stop, if you want." He pulled a small Bible from his pocket and laid it in his lap.

Kellie waited to see what Angie would do. The girl stared at the book, fingers trembling, eyes blinking nervously. Finally she gave Ted a defiant look. "I'm not interested, thanks. Mom, I'm going to bed. Good night."

Kellie watched her friend leave. Ted sat waiting. She understood Angie's reluctance, but was desperate for a normal life again. "OK, Ted, I'll listen."

"You guys can use the kitchen," Mrs. Hollis suggested. "I'll wait here and read."

Heading to the back of the house, Kellie wished

Mitch were home. She didn't want to face this alone. What was Ted planning to do? Did he really think a Bible could stop "ghosts" from banging on walls and severed heads from appearing out of nowhere?

He sat on the opposite side of the kitchen table and laid the Bible open, sliding it toward her. "Read out loud, please."

"What?" she asked.

"Genesis 1:1. The beginning."

Her eyes scanned the page. She felt enraged at his request, yet didn't really understand why. Glancing at the doorway, she considered leaving.

Ted waited patiently and then pointed to the first paragraph, bringing her attention back to the book. "Here," he said gently.

Slowly she read out loud how God created the world, Adam and Eve, and the animals, only to have a snake ruin everything. After a while she paused. "What does this have to do with me?"

Ted explained that it was the snake, or Satan, and his demonic angels, rather than ghosts, who were scaring her with their appearances, noises, and the rest. And he told her about Jesus. "It's *important* that you understand something," he stressed. "The Bible tells us that because Jesus died on the cross and then rose from the dead, He was given *all* authority in heaven and earth.* That means He has authority over you, over me, and most important, over Satan and his demon angels."

"That's all great," she sighed. "But what exactly am I supposed to *do*? I need real help!"

Ted smiled. "Kellie, I'm offering you real help!

Right now Satan's running your life. But if you'll read the Bible and start praying to Jesus every day, God will start running your life instead, and He'll protect you from Satan's attacks. As for what else you can do, I want you to get rid of anything that gives Satan an excuse to bug you. Then find a church."

"You want me to throw things away?"

"Yes. Toss out books, music, posters . . . anything that glorifies death, ghosts, witchcraft, or immorality. If you've got any drugs or alcohol, dump them in the sewer. Getting high won't make you see or hear demons, but it does open the door to it. If you own a Ouija board, get rid of it! And don't just throw it away . . . burn it."

After that, he led Kellie in her first real prayer. It felt awkward, like a new pair of shoes. Each word, each phrase—a baby step. When she asked Jesus to be her Savior, a new peace settled in her heart, taking away a noticeable measure of the dark panic she'd carried there for so many years.

When she finished, he gave her a quick, gentle hug. "Here, take this with you tonight," he said, handing her his own Bible.

"Why?"

"Because you'll need it, and I can always get another one. Read it before you go to bed. Sleep with it if you feel scared. If Satan attacks you in the middle of the night, call out the name of Jesus . . . the second you do, Satan *has* to flee, because he's no match for Jesus' power. And when the attack is over, read the Bible some more." He paused to offer a reassuring smile. "Kellie, you're in for some rough battles; Satan won't let you go without a fight. But Jesus will have the victory. The demons will flee, and your life will go back to normal . . . I promise."

Then he wrote out a prayer for her to say at bed-time and in the morning until she got comfortable praying from her heart.

For the first time in years Kellie felt real hope that the nightmare would soon end and her future would begin.

_____
* See Matthew 28:18.

Chapter 17

Into Battle

Back in the guesthouse Kellie spent an uneasy night hugging her new Bible. Her years of dabbling in the occult were over, but as Ted had warned, the attacks were not . . . at least not yet. Sleep came in brief snatches, sandwiched between fresh waves of Satan's gripping, paralyzing presence.

Now that she had the truth—knew who lived behind the mask of all those ghostly pranks—Satan was coming at her for all he was worth, revealing his full true nature at last. No more sending helpful "ghosts" to smile at her in friendship. No more bothering to make her feel special or watched over. He knew she saw through his crafty games. Consequently, each attack was worse than the one before, leaving her exhausted from the struggle. Like the time she'd almost drowned in Beaver Lake, evil's grip made it hard for her to breathe, almost impossible for her to speak.

It was nearly dawn when Kellie found herself

caught in the struggle again, this time without even falling asleep first. Her eyes were open; the dark room appeared to be lit with an unearthly light, the walls vibrating as if alive. She struggled to sit up, but something, no, *someone* with an evil face was sitting on her chest, holding her down like a rag doll. She tried calling Jesus' name . . . a mere whisper of the letter J was all that came out. Again she tried and failed. On her third try she gave it her all, straining, pushing, until sound broke through the involuntary silence. "Jesus . . ." she breathed out the name, desperate for relief. "Jesus!" she cried louder, then felt everything instantly change. The dark, menacing presence fled, releasing her. The room went back to normal. It was over.

Kellie decided she'd had enough. She looked out the window and saw dawn breaking over the mountains. She turned on the light and read Ted's Bible until the sun rose high enough to chase away the darkness. Then she slept peacefully until hunger gently woke her for the day.

After breakfast she gave her life a good spiritual sweeping. She tossed out rock music tapes, scary books, and her statue of Buddha. She flushed the last of her pot down the toilet. Finally she took the Ouija board into the main house and burned it in the fireplace. It surprised her that throwing away so many treasures didn't hurt. Instead, it felt wonderful. She just wished she could do the same with her parents' pagan idols, but they weren't hers to destroy.

That night she told them the news of her newfound faith. Kellie's dad listened indulgently as she explained the years of frightening experiences and how

Ted had led her to God. "I don't care what you choose to believe," he said, laughing bitterly. "Just don't try selling it to me."

Her mom was less amused. "Kellie, I had no idea you were going through all that. But why *church*? What will that do?" She shook her head. "Well, it's your life. I won't stand in your way."

When Kellie told Tommy, he predicted a short run. "It won't last, Squirt. I give you and religion six months, tops."

Ellen was skeptical too, but was more worried about her own kids than Kellie's spiritual life.

Her family's attitude stung. She hoped her friends would be more supportive, but they failed her as well. Sara had long since left the party scene and was in favor of whatever might chase the "ghosts" away, but had no room in her own life for God. Kellie's other lake friends, including Amy and Angie, refused to listen at all and taunted her with vicious names for refusing to party with them anymore.

Telling Mitch was the hardest of all. Deep down, she'd secretly hoped he'd be interested in learning more, maybe even be willing to walk with her in her new life. But he too angrily accused her of betrayal and walked away. It broke her heart to lose him. But the price of winning him back was simply too high. She would not offend God and could not face Satan without Jesus at her side. That meant letting go.

Over the next few days the nightly attacks came less often. When she told Ted the good news, he told her to go find a church. Kellie wanted to go, but still didn't own a car. She knew Mrs. Hollis was a sober member of AA and approved of Kellie's desire to change, so she asked her to take them church visiting. Mrs. Hollis agreed. She and Kellie tried a small nearby church first. The people were nice, but the sanctuary was stuffy and hot, and Kellie had a hard time understanding the sermon. They left as soon as it was over.

The next Sunday, they chose a Catholic church several miles from the lake. The building was dark and musty inside, with sad-looking statues and paintings. The long, formal service made Kellie uncomfortable. It felt nothing like what she remembered in Mexico.

Finally they tried a large community church in the San Fernando Valley, known for its lively services. Everything was fine until about halfway through the sermon when the pastor told everyone to gather in groups to pray. Their prayers came out in a strange language, and many began weeping and wailing, arms waving wildly about. Kellie and Mrs. Hollis locked eyes in confusion then burst out laughing. Not wanting to offend anyone, they hurried out.

"Can't you find me a church?" Kellie asked Ted in frustration. She was tired of church shopping. "You could try the Adventist church where I go sometimes," he said. "They're friendly, and they stick to the Bible."

He offered to take her that next Saturday. Sabbath

morning Kellie dressed in her favorite jeans and top. As usual, she covered her ears, neck, arms, fingers, ankles, and toes with silver jewelry to look her best. At the church Kellie confessed her butterflies to Ted. "What if this one isn't right either? I might never find a church."

"Just give it a chance. You might be surprised."

They sat near the back of the softly lit sanctuary. There were no statues or paintings, only plants. Kellie stood along with the others when the music started, but didn't know the words. An elderly woman sitting nearby noticed and offered a hymnal, already open to the right song. The pastor's sermon was clear and easy to follow. Best of all, no one melted into hysterics during the prayer.

"You were right . . . I like this place," she told Ted afterward. "It *feels* right."

He smiled. "If you want, we can stay for potluck, meet the pastor."

"What's potluck?" she asked.

He muffled a belly laugh. "You'll see! And you'll love it, I promise."

Kellie spent the next hour eating delicious homemade food and getting to know the friendliest people she'd ever met. She also noticed how simply the women dressed, making her suddenly aware of her many accessories, dark makeup, and clothes that were more skimpy than stylish. Somewhat embarrassed, she kept expecting someone to comment on her appearance, but no one ever did. They only asked if she'd enjoyed the service and if she'd be there next Sabbath.

For the first time in her life Kellie happily soaked

in the true love and kindness of God's people first-hand. It felt wonderfully warm and safe.

"I think this is the one," she later told Ted. "I can't wait to come back."

Chapter 18

Final
Victory

Over the next several months Kellie's mom helped out by combining her own errands with dropping Kellie off for church. After just a few times she agreed to help Kellie buy her first used car.

In time, Kellie found a job and signed up for night classes at the community college. Her run-ins with Satan came less frequently but did not stop altogether. Some nights nothing happened, but on others he attacked with as much fury as ever. She tried to be patient, but she really wanted to be left alone *now*, for good. Ashamed and feeling like a failure, she avoided telling Ted about it.

Meanwhile she found several sober friends her age to hang out with, including a boy named Don. He was tall and lean, with thick black hair and brooding dark eyes that somehow managed to light up when he smiled. He was quirky and adventuresome, lots of fun to be with.

On an especially crisp October day she and Don spent the day exploring various buildings in Hollywood. The last one looked like a castle, with heavy stonework and gargoyles. A crew was filming a movie there, so no one noticed their poking around.

It was all great fun until a scary-looking man with a gun in a shoulder holster got aboard the elevator they were riding. "Are you lost?" he demanded to know.

"No, just exploring," Don said.

The man scowled and told them they were trespassing in the Church of Scientology headquarters, home of the famous cult founded by L. Ron Hubbard.

Back in the car Kellie laughed. "Wow, was that a wrong turn or what? I'm glad I've already found a church."

"Me too. But you still don't seem very happy. Is something wrong?"

"I haven't been sleeping much," she said, relieved to admit it. "I thought Satan would be leaving me alone by now."

Don flashed a knowing smile. "I have an idea!" he said. "Someone told me about a meeting tonight. It's supposed to help people with spiritual stuff. We can go if you want."

Kellie thought about it. She knew Ted wouldn't approve. But she couldn't run to him with every spiritual decision that came along. "OK, I'll go," she agreed.

When they got there, the meeting was just starting. They paid a young woman the fee and explained why they'd come.

She smiled sympathetically. "I'm sure we can help," she said. "Someone will talk to you after the meeting."

They took the last two seats along the back wall, Kellie beside a middle-aged woman with red hair. She turned to Kellie and smiled. "Hello, I'm Tanya. Are you having problems with spirits, dear?"

"How'd you know?"

"It shows," she said, patting Kellie's knee. "Don't worry. Tonight's speaker will know what to do."

Kellie felt uncomfortable. She should have run this by Ted after all. She was about to leave when the speaker asked for everyone's attention. Not wishing to be rude, Kellie stayed put. The speaker asked if anyone wanted a bigger house or newer car. She waved a Bible and wrote verses on the blackboard. "I'm going to show you how to use white magic, a mixture of incantations and Bible principles, to get whatever you desire."

The Bible reassured Kellie somewhat, but the mention of magic was alarming.

When the speaker finished, she came right over to Kellie. "Hi, I'm Cassandra. I understand you need to get rid of some demons?"

Kellie stared at the older woman, wondering how this stranger could know about demons.

Tanya took Kellie's hand. "If you'll come with us, dear, we'll help you."

Kellie looked to Don for rescue, but he offered none. "Go ahead," he said. "I'll wait here."

She felt outnumbered by these odd women, but decided to follow them anyway. They entered a small room in the back. "Here," Tanya gently urged, "just lie down on the table, and we'll pray over you." Then she closed the door and dimmed the lights while Cassandra lit candles.

After Kellie closed her eyes, the women chanted and "prayed" over her, passing their hands inches from her face, torso, and legs in long sweeping movements until Kellie got too uncomfortable to stay quiet. "I feel dizzy," she complained. "And my skin is hot."

"That's the positive energy we're giving you," Cassandra explained. "It will protect you."

Something inside Kellie told her this wasn't right. She opened her eyes to make them stop, but they were already done.

"Let me help you up," Tanya offered. She held out a helping hand, reminding Kellie of the demon who had once "helped" her out of bed.

Kellie's body tingled, and her mind felt fuzzy. She shook her head to clear the cobwebs.

"It takes a minute to adjust," Cassandra explained. "Now let me tell you what you'll need to do at home tonight to clear out any remaining spirits."

Outside, Kellie repeated their instructions to Don. "They want you to burn herbs in a cast-iron skillet and carry it around the edge of the guesthouse?"

"Yeah. Here are the herbs. I'm supposed to chant, too."

She was reluctant, but he convinced her to try

it. When they were finished, he left. It didn't take long for her to fall asleep. But before she could start dreaming, Satan attacked her with alarming strength and intensity. The meeting had been a terrible mistake. She'd stepped right into his trap! "I'm sorry, God," she silently prayed. "Please help me!"

It took longer than usual to speak Jesus' name, but as always, the sound brought instant relief. Kellie immediately called Ted and told him everything.

He gasped through the phone lines. "You did *what*? Why?"

"I don't know. They had a Bible. Don thought it would help."

"OK, I'll pray with you now, but tomorrow we have work to do."

The next day he showed her Galatians 5:19-21, 2 Chronicles 33:6, and Deuteronomy 18:9-13, Bible verses that warned against witchcraft of any kind. Then he led her through several prayers, renouncing the occult and asking God to forgive her for turning to witches, white magic, and incantations instead of trusting Him. Then he ordered Satan and his demons to leave the guesthouse and asked God to send the Holy Spirit and His holy angels to guard and protect it. Ted's prayer reminded her of the angels that had fought over her before. Only now, the dark angel was banished for good.

The next Sabbath she told the senior pastor what had happened and asked his advice. He suggested weekly Bible study at the home of the associate pastor and his wife, Becky.

Kellie relished her time with the sweet young couple. They taught her godly principles and led her to a time of decision. In the end it wasn't hard. The plain church with the friendly people had become her second home and family. She wanted to belong.

Chapter 19

Second Birth

On a clear April Sabbath Kellie calmly entered the baptismal water with six other new believers as sunlight streamed through the stained-glass window above. After her body adjusted to the tepid water, she took a moment to carefully scan the people sitting in the sanctuary. There were so many—people of every imaginable age and race. There was Ted, off in his usual corner, grinning from ear to ear, with Mrs. Hollis at his side. The associate pastor sat up front with Becky, who caught Kellie's eye and waved. Finally she spotted her. Kellie's mom sat near the back, alone, quietly showing support for her daughter's choice to serve God.

Kellie remembered the day she'd told her mom of her decision.

"Are you sure this is what you want?" she'd asked.

"Yes. I know you don't understand, Mom, but having Jesus in my life just makes everything so much

better. It's like He's always *right there*, ready to listen
or help me out of a jam, or protect me when I'm
scared. I can't live without Him."

"You're right; I don't understand. And your dad
thinks you're ruining your life." She paused to gently
move a stray hair out of Kellie's eyes. "Listen, all I
know is that I've never seen you happier or calmer.
You've quit all the partying, you're holding down a
job, and your friends are nicer people. So if you tell
me that all that happened because of God and church,
I'm all for it."

The memory warmed Kellie's heart. It would take
time, but she felt certain that that conversation had
been just the first step toward building a loving rela-
tionship with her mom. Maybe they'd even be friends
one day, and *maybe* her mom would accept Christ.

The senior pastor placed a gentle hand on her
shoulder, bringing her attention back to the task at
hand. She felt a sudden thrill. It was her turn to pub-
licly give up her old life forever.

"Kellie, do you accept Jesus as your Lord and
Savior?"

"I do."

The pastor covered her nose and mouth, and she
willingly slipped into the waters at the mercy of another. But then swift, strong arms brought her back
again, entering her into a new life of freedom, love,
and the peaceful contentment she'd sought for years.
Standing upright, she felt darkness fall away from her
like an old skin, making room for a great light. She
was a new creation, like a baby just born.

It had come at a terrible cost: she'd lost friends,

the respect of family, and the option to follow her own selfish plans. Living for God would not always be easy. Even so, the price was small compared to all she'd gained, especially Jesus.

In that moment she thought back on all she'd gone through. Had God always known she'd some-day give her heart to Jesus? Was that why He'd saved her life again and again, and sent a holy angel to fight for her before she even knew she'd need it?

Just then one of the girls who'd been baptized gave Kellie a hug. "Isn't this great?" she beamed.

Kellie grinned back, certain the two would some-day be friends. "I searched for God my *whole life*. Finding Him makes this the best day ever."

"And surely I am with you always, to the very end of the age." *

---

* Matthew 28:20.